THE DIRTY DAYS

The DIRTY DAYS

A Young Girl's Journey to and
from the Oklahoma Dust Bowl

NORMA WELTY
A Novel Based on Her Life

iUniverse, Inc.
Bloomington

The Dirty Days
A Young Girl's Journey to and from the Oklahoma Dust Bowl

iUniverse books may be ordered through booksellers or by contacting:

iUniverse
1663 Liberty Drive
Bloomington, IN 47403
www.iuniverse.com
1-800-Authors (1-800-288-4677)

Cover photo: Author and her younger sister sitting on a visiting neighbor's car the day after a dust storm.

ISBN: 978-1-4759-3150-1 (sc)
ISBN: 978-1-4759-3148-8 (hc)
ISBN: 978-1-4759-3149-5 (e)

Library of Congress Control Number: 2012910098

Printed in the United States of America

iUniverse rev. date: 06/19/2012

To the 1930s' Dust Bowl children and their courageous parents who persevered until it became a better time and place.

—Norma Welty

Acknowledgments

Thanks to my siblings Sue, Jane, and Bill for their excitement about this book; my deceased brothers, JR and Kenneth, who I know would wish me the best if they could; my husband, Robert, for all the times he loaded and unloaded the dishwasher and for not complaining about our frequent deli dinners or restaurant takeouts; my grandson, Aaron, for his interest in my oral stories of his ancestors' survival in the Dust Bowl and for saying, "Keep on writing, Grandmother"; my son, Dan, for his enthusiastic encouragement and for being so proud of me; my daughter, Ginger, for her expertise, excellent judgment, and heartfelt support, which helped put me over the finish line; and my cousin La Verne in Arkansas for her inspirational telephone visits and her search for pictures.

I'm especially grateful to Wynell, a longtime friend and classmate in Oklahoma. Anytime I had a question or just felt the need to reminisce about our time and place, I could always count on her energetic interest in my project.

I also wish to extend my sincere thanks to my editor, Helga Schier, for her respectful editing and evaluation. Her suggestions and insight made this a better book.

Author's Message

With knowledge that readers don't clamor for memoirs written by unknowns, I struggled for two years attempting to write this book. Finally I came to a crossroad, and I needed to make a choice. One path led to my making time for many more solitary hours a day toiling at my writing task—for who knew how many more years. The other offered an enticingly familiar scene: I could return to a time when I had known a relatively comfortable life as a full-time homemaker with adequate quality time left over for recreation, family, and friends.

Ironically, it was family and the few friends who knew I was writing this book who urged me not to give up my project. One friend, a university professor, pointed out that my story of victory over hard times embodies the universality to which all humankind can relate. So heeding the input, I continued to write, discard, and rewrite. Finally I concluded that I simply wasn't comfortable using the many unavoidable *I*'s necessary in a memoir that were calling attention to me, Norma Welty, an unknown writer. Then a solution came to me. I would call on my alter ego, a creative self, to narrate my story. Hence, an imaginary Molly, also an elderly woman, would tell my story with much more creativity and ease, and my book would be a novel instead of a memoir.

At that juncture, I began to write with intense vigor, and soon it was apparent my story had taken on a life of its own. When I finished my manuscript and family and close friends congratulated me, I confided that it had been an experience of both agony and ecstasy. This is what I didn't tell them: the agony had been the physical and mental drain due to the mechanics of getting my best language skills on paper without flaws or typos galore. The ecstasy had come from my keen awareness of my story's heartbeat.

So, I invite you, dear reader, to take a journey into the lives of courageous folks and their kind benefactors. Yes, all are unknowns as individuals, but I hope their ultimate victory over the well-known hardships in the Dust Bowl during the 1930s will make your trip through this book a meaningful experience.

Chapter One

It was moving day! Mother was not entirely happy, and only a few hours before she had said to me, "It's an ambitious plan for such hard times. Pulling up stakes here and all and moving on to Oklahoma. Oh, I pray about it considerably."

Still, excitement was in the air, and my own earlier twinge of anxiety about moving from our home in Arkansas vanished. Mother also tried to do her part in propelling the excitement. She glanced mischievously at Daddy while softly singing "My Old Kentucky Home," changing the lyrics to Arkansas. Daddy almost skipped as he moved about, even when Maribelle, his youthful step-grandmother, stopped over to say good-bye.

Mother, Daddy, and I scurried about packing the back of the old truck with our possessions piled high above the sideboard extensions Daddy had built himself. He grinned and said, "Hey, Molly May Dowden, my nearly seven-year-old, make yourself useful and keep this here rope from tangling up while I tie our stuff down so's it won't fall off once we get on the road." He soon finished securing our belongings, and we were quickly on our way.

After all three of us had been jostled about inside the cab of the truck, bumping and careening down the rugged mountain road, we were soon relieved to be on a smooth highway—a new road that would take us to a whole new world.

I was sitting in the middle, and I could see Daddy's white-knuckle grip on the steering wheel relax as he peered over my head and said, "Well, Elsa Ruth, here we are on our way, with our cash stashed."

Mother responded, "Yes, Tillman. We're on our way! Oklahoma, here we come!"

I liked it when Mother and Daddy joked. However, Daddy's mention of the cash caused me to worry. I'd heard Mother say it was coming up on four years since the stock market crash of 1929 had caused bad times for many folks, and some people were doing desperate things just to survive.

She'd also told Daddy—when she didn't know I was listening—about a bank robber named Pretty Boy Floyd who sometimes hung out in eastern Oklahoma. I intended to help my parents watch out for him once we crossed over into Oklahoma because I worried he might rob travelers, too. I was afraid he would guess our money was hidden inside one of our mattresses.

The money was from Daddy's step-grandmother, Maribelle—a cash settlement in exchange for our leaving the Arkansas farm that had belonged to Daddy's deceased Grandpa Dowden. She wanted her brother to take over the farming of the land, instead of Daddy. Daddy took Maribelle's offer—the cash and her old truck—and his vision of a better future was sweetened. And so we were on our way.

After several delays from oil leaks, flat tires, a broken fan belt, a leaking radiator, engine problems, and sleeping nights upright in the cab of the truck, it seemed we had been on the road for weeks. But my concerns about Pretty Boy Floyd and our numerous truck issues were nothing compared to the encounter we were about to have with a dust storm about a hundred miles west of Oklahoma City.

~

As the dust engulfed us, I recalled that before we left Arkansas, Daddy had casually told us that Oklahoma had seen a number of dust storms that late winter and early spring. But there was nothing casual about the nature of this particular dust storm, nor any of the others we were destined to experience in the years to come.

Before long the dust storm made me cough; Daddy was coughing, too. Mother, blinking her eyes from the dirt all around us in the air, nervously cautioned, "We seem to be the only vehicle on the road."

"I know it," Daddy acknowledged. "I can't tell the road from the ditch. I saw a little old gas station about ten miles back with a cafe. Did y'all see it a little bit this side of some dinky burg of a town? A little ways back?"

Mother said she'd noticed, and Daddy said he was going to turn the truck around and go back. Turning the truck around in the blinding dust without going into the ditch wasn't easy. But Daddy did the job well, and we soon were glad to be rolling with the wind instead of against it.

~

Two cars were parked right in front of the cafe, and we had to park next to a third car along the side. Getting from the truck to the cafe door was a feat to remember. The wind flattened me as soon as my feet were on the ground, and Daddy picked me up and carried me. Mother, nearly blinded by the dust, walked close behind Daddy with her arms clamped around his waist. At times the wind's force caused them to gain a step and then lose a step, and it was a genuine struggle for them to get to the cafe door without losing me. But fear had bolstered our inclination to cling to each other, and we finally lunged through the cafe door in one clump. Several heads turned toward us in understandable surprise.

Two other families were taking shelter in the dingy cafe as well, bringing the total to eleven customers all together; add the owner, and there were twelve people in the room. Everyone was holding a wet rag over nose and mouth, and right away the owner of the place tore three pieces from a dish towel, wet them, and gave us ours. A few minutes later a thirteenth person—a hitchhiker, or tramp, as homeless people were generally called then—flung the door open with the help of the wind and stumbled into the cafe. The owner gave him a damp rag, too.

~

We had arrived at the cafe around three in the afternoon, and everyone endured near silence for what seemed like an eternity. It was an awkward situation at best, but we were a group of brow-creasing strangers with wet cloths covering our noses and mouths. Talking was nearly impossible, but at least we were inside. At suppertime the owner served us a family-style meal of chili, red beans, onions, and corn bread. When we finished eating, he waved away anyone who tried to pay him. He simply motioned toward an empty glass jar on the counter and said, "If any of y'all want to leave a few pennies in that jar there, you can. But if you can't, you can't. Don't worry about it."

With humble demeanor, the tramp responded, "Sir, I can stay around for a few hours when this here dust storm is over and clean up the dust for you."

The owner thanked him for his thoughtful offer, and he said, "The food woulda hada be throwed away anyway. Tomorrow'll be Sunday, and I ain't open Sundays. Besides that, I reckon the ice man heard a dust storm was on its way, and he didn't deliver ice today. And things'll be gone bad by Monday anyways."

"It's awful nice of him to treat the tramp so respectfully," Mother whispered to Daddy. "I've read that tramps these days are usually family men out trying to find work." I felt sorry for the man, and I was glad Daddy wasn't a tramp.

Mother and the other women cleared the tables and washed the dishes. When everything was done, our host turned on the radio and we listened to the famous Carter Family singing toe-tapping gospel songs from Nashville. I'd heard them sing on a phonograph record at Maribelle and Great-Grandpa Dowden's once, and it was exciting to hear them on the radio. But intermittent static spoiled our listening pleasure, and so the owner soon turned off the radio.

"None too soon," Mother said quietly. "I imagine all of us are worn out from the strain of all this." She was right. We all seemed ready to pack it in.

"The toilet's not working right—wants to overflow," the owner announced as he was about to go to his cot in a back room, "and I'll put a bucket in there so's y'all won't haf tuh go to the outdoors toilet in the storm."

I saw Mother roll her eyes slightly, and at the same time a frail-looking boy about eleven years old caught my attention when he said, "Mama, I'll be too scared to go in there in the dark."

The owner heard the boy and assured him that he would leave the indoor cafe lanterns burning low all night so people could find their way.

By then all of us, the families and the tramp, had found spaces on the floor of the kitchen and the small dining area and settled down for some sleep, still clinging to those damp cloths over our faces. That is, until we were startled out of our wits by the screams of a woman, followed instantly by a strange whacking sound.

It turned out it wasn't a woman's scream after all. It was the high-pitched squeal of the frail-looking boy. When his mother asked him what had happened, he held his inner wrist close to her face and choked, "Something bit me right here."

A man standing next to the injured child pointed to a very large crumpled centipede lying about two feet from the boy and said, "When I heard the young feller yell, I looked over and I seen the longest old centipede I'd ever seen in my life. And the closest weapon I had was my hat, and I whapped the dern thing with it."

We all stretched our necks to see the centipede; some stepped over for a closer look at the black-bodied, yellow-legged intruder. Each of us swore it was at least nine inches long. One woman bent low for a better look and blurted, "Merciful heavens, I saw it quiver. Hit it with your shoe or something!"

The man who had zapped the centipede assured her it was dead. But he layered several paper napkins in his hand, picked up the lifeless creature, struggled to open the door to a blast of dust, and threw it outside.

As soon as everyone had settled down, the owner said, "Centipedes hardly ever bite humans, but lately over to the northwest in the panhandle and places not far from there, centipedes has been coming into homes and businesses in droves during dust storms." He looked around as if he were expecting someone to comment. No one did, and he continued, "Looks like now they's gonna to be pestering us, too." Everyone nodded. And he suddenly seemed to realize time was fleeing, and he turned toward the kitchen saying, "I gotta go now and fix up something to hep this here chile."

At that point Mother leaned close to Daddy and whispered, "He talks as much like a hillbilly as some of the folks on the mountain."

"A centipede's venom's only a large enough amount to kill insects for food, not to take out a human," said the tramp while stepping forward to fill the silence left by the owner, who had disappeared into the kitchen. "But that one's a real big one, and its bite would hurt a boy his size real bad."

The tramp apparently had forgotten the child's mother would hear his remark. But she did, and it didn't soothe her.

While she caressed her son's hair and cheeks, her silent tears made tracks through the dust on her face, already smudged by the damp cloth. The boy's father furtively swiped a tear from his cheekbone with the back of his fist while he comforted his wife and son. I felt my eyes getting watery, too. I deeply regretted that I was too shy to talk to the distraught family and say I was sorry, like some folks and one older child had done. Mother and Daddy talked to them, too, and Mother promised she'd pray for the boy's quick recovery. The others echoed her words, also promising to keep the boy in their prayers.

Soon the owner returned with a pan of warm, soapy water mixed with a few drops of ammonia and washed the boy's wound with the smelly mixture. After the first-aid treatment, the boy vomited into the pan. "I expected that," the owner said to calm the mother's rising fears. "Centipede bites kin bring that on. Here's a cup of ginger tea I made in case you'd need it. It's been said it quells the puking. Here, boy, aspirin for your pain, too."

The youngster soon fell asleep, and the rest of us slept, too. By morning the boy appeared paler, and his mother approached my mother and confided, "He does feel better, but he has a scary-looking yellow fluid sack around the puncture on his wrist."

"Oh, I'm sorry to hear that. But it's probably a normal reaction. You might want to take him to a doctor, though," Mother sympathized.

The father indicated that his son wanted to lie low. So we all readily gave him his space and hurried toward the restroom door, where we stood in line waiting to use the makeshift toilet. Then we waited in line again to get into the kitchen, where the owner had invited us to wash our hands and faces before we ate the breakfast he had set out for us.

After two bites of the leftover corn bread with applesauce, my stomach felt queasy, and I was glad the injured boy was sleeping and wouldn't have to eat the dry corn bread and overly sweet applesauce. But it seemed like everyone else enjoyed the breakfast. And, although the owner had neglected to put a container on the counter for our payment, I was glad to see Daddy and another man leave some money on a table.

~

The dust storm moved on by mid-morning. Daddy shoveled away the knee-high pile of dust that had drifted against the outside door so the owner could get out and put some gas in our truck and add water to the radiator.

After Daddy paid the owner for the gas and thanked him for

the water, he and Mother said their polite good-byes to everyone, and the three of us headed toward our truck.

"He may not be running a legal eating place, with no working indoor toilet and all. Ha, I bet it never has worked," Mother said as soon as we were in the truck with the doors closed. "Still, that man's a bighearted person," she continued. Daddy and I nodded in agreement, although I was surprised to hear that the man might have told a lie when he said the toilet wasn't working. I certainly thought he was a very kind man, and I sure hoped he was being truthful.

Still feeling travel-worn, we drove on. I was looking forward to sleeping in a real bed, and I was sure my folks were, too. After two nights of sleeping in the truck and the third on the hard floor of the cafe, I thought a bed would be a luxury. So with only a few more hours of travel ahead of us, I put my mind on sleeping in a soft bed with sheets, quilts, and a pillow in what I hoped would be a dust-free home.

Thinking about sleeping in a nice bed should have caused me to feel drowsy, but my mind wouldn't stop thinking. I wondered how long it would be before I would again see Mother's parents, Grandpa and Grandma Dryden. I hoped Daddy's older cousins, where we would be staying in Oklahoma, would seem a little like them. I had loved Grandma's cooking and Grandpa's singing or playing the fiddle while Mother's brothers and sisters sang religious and folk songs, later called bluegrass. My mind took me back to the family songfests and the one time we went to a barn dance to hear my grandpa and family play and sing. I felt my foot wanting to tap to the rhythm, but the urge didn't last. The monotonous sound of the old truck's engine soon took over again.

~

As we drove, Mother dozed. Daddy stared at the road, hardly blinking. But then a sudden thud underneath the truck caused all three of us to jump.

"What was that?" Mother asked, eyes wide open with alarm.

"Oh, a dad gum jackrabbit jumped right in front of me. Came from out of nowhere on the right-hand side! Now he's dead as a doornail," Daddy answered, shaking his head.

The thud had jolted me right out of my imaginary soft and clean bed and my thoughts about my mother's family and back to reality, and I instantly visualized another long delay caused by more truck problems. But my worry lasted only a split second. We drove on without losing a bit of time, and I quickly peeked around Daddy's head to the left side of the road and saw the poor, dead rabbit's companions hopping across the vast, flat land. They didn't seem to know that something terrible had just happened.

I couldn't stop feeling sad about the rabbit whose hopping days were over. My folks must have felt the sadness, too. Then after a long silence Daddy took a deep breath, peered at Mother over the top of my head, and said, "Well, Elsa Ruth, here we are still heading west with our cash still stashed."

"Yes, Tillman. Here we are in Oklahoma, and I imagine some folks in Oklahoma are hankering to be heading west, too. Only they want to go to California."

Never missing a chance to worry, I wondered if very many people would be leaving Oklahoma. Judging by what I'd seen from the truck window, it looked like there might not be very many children, and I wanted to have lots of friends in school. But I appreciated my folks' humor—if Mother's comments were truly meant to be funny.

Chapter Two

"That's gotta be their house right up yonder," Daddy informed us, pointing to a large farmhouse about a half mile up the road.

"I'll bet it is," Mother replied, "and, Molly May, that reminds me to tell you that Clifford and Milly Sue Bridges are probably near sixty years old. We're still in our twenties, and you're a child."

Daddy's head snapped around toward Mother, and I saw the puzzled look on his face.

"So we'll need to call them Mr. and Mrs. Bridges out of respect," Mother continued, ignoring Daddy's look. "For sure we respect them for taking us in."

Daddy nodded in agreement, and I promised myself that I'd give them the respect they deserved, and perhaps even a bit more if only I'd get to sleep in that cozy bed I couldn't stop thinking about.

~

Mr. and Mrs. Bridges welcomed us cordially. Unlike all the dreary, unpainted houses we'd seen along the last fifty miles of road, theirs was painted a nice shade of yellow on the outside, and it had very pleasant wallpaper and furnishings on the inside. Mrs. Bridges seemed exceptionally pleased we were there. She took us to our bedrooms and asked Mr. Bridges to bring heated bathwater for the tubs that sat in the corners of our rooms.

Before we bathed, Mother took all our clothes outside and tried to shake out the dust that had sifted into the boxes we had packed them in for our journey. Then she and I bathed and put on what barely passed as clean clothing. I felt refreshed anyway. Mother took me downstairs to the kitchen, where Mrs. Bridges was preparing a fine supper. While she busied herself with the cooking, she kept asking questions about our journey. Listening to Mother tell about the troublesome, time-consuming flat tires and mechanical problems with the truck took my mind back to the three of us sleeping in the truck in a sitting position. I felt cramped and squirmy just recalling how jammed together on the truck's seat we had been, hoping the two down-filled quilts would keep our body heat in tow.

Soon, as my eyes followed the steaming bowls of food being carried to the dining room table, I imagined another kind of warmth. I could hardly wait to have my fill and then crawl into the wonderfully warm softness waiting for me in the bed of Mr. and Mrs. Bridges's grown-up daughter.

Yes, all of this was awesome for travel-weary me, and I felt like shouting, using words I knew Mother would say. We've journeyed far from the lush green of our birth state to this vast beige land and this large and pretty home, our wonderful new world!

But little did my young mind imagine that in time it would feel as if we were minor actors on a stage where the weather would be the villain and his costar the disabled economy.

~

At breakfast the next morning, Mr. Bridges talked about dust storms. I'd been through one already and felt I knew all I wanted to know about them, so I didn't really listen until he said dust storms had been worse in nearby Cimarron County. Animals and birds had died, and a number of people, especially small children, had become sick with very bad coughs and lung infections from breathing in the dust. I had no idea a dust storm could make you sick, and I very much hoped the farm we'd soon move to wouldn't be in Cimarron County.

I liked listening to Mr. and Mrs. Bridges talk about their recent life in the southwest, but I was even more eager to hear about their lives when they were younger. But as always, I was too shy to ask questions. I did, however, learn from listening that they had been in their late teens when their families settled on adjoining land in the 1893 Oklahoma Land Rush, which, I gathered, had something to do with the government giving away land to those who claimed it. All of that was very long ago to me, and I liked finding out that southwest Oklahoma had been lived in for a long while, and I hoped people soon would have time to plant some trees that would grow tall and wide and give some shade.

Mother threw in questions I would have liked to ask, and I heard about young Clifford and Milly Sue's wedding soon after their families began farming on their claims. I was sad to learn that shortly after they were married, their parents, all four of them, died within a few weeks.

"'Twas smallpox. That sickness spread to young and old those days—still does to the young. Started on the Indian reservations, so people say, anyway," Mr. Bridges informed us. Then he said, "Now, where was I—oh, I know. And two farms were left to me and Milly. We were just a young couple that didn't know a dang thing about farming in these parts," confided Mr. Bridges at the end of his story.

When Mother and Daddy sympathized politely, Mrs. Bridges interjected, "Our neighbor, Mr. Bradshaw, he had a wife who died of smallpox, too. Left Mr. Bradshaw with a lot of land, some of it better'n ours. You see, he ended up with her folks' land and his folks' land, just like us. You can see their big spread from our back porch."

Mother and Daddy shook their heads and said they worried about smallpox still being around and that they hoped Mr. Bradshaw was doing all right alone on such a big farm.

"Well, he stayed a widower until ten years ago when he married his first wife's cousin, a younger lady from Dallas. They begot themselves a daughter. Helen Marie, her name is, and a little older than your Molly May here. They made a lot of money before the drought and dust storms started, like so many did who had inherited a lot of land. And they don't want for nothing. Nothing that money can buy, anyway."

~

Daddy's work as a farmhand and overseer of the upcoming cotton harvest on the large Bridges farm would be in exchange for our lodging in one of the two-room cotton pickers' shanties, some farm-raised foods, and five dollars a month in wages. With that, plus Mother's small change for doing Mrs. Bridges's laundry, feeding and watering the chickens, and other miscellaneous tasks, my folks figured we could manage well enough. But soon we found out that adequate food and lodging weren't all we'd need for creature comforts.

On our second day on the farm, another serious dust storm

hit. We had moved into the workers' shanty, but we hadn't had time to buy any staples such as flour, cornmeal, rice, or potatoes to add to the small supply of canned goods we had brought with us from Arkansas. So Mr. and Mrs. Bridges insisted we come for supper and spend the night with them under more comfortable conditions.

When I heard them invite us to stay in their house again, I was scarcely able to suppress my urge to clap with joy. I was eager to bask in the luxury of their large, comfortable house. Imagining the huge, tasty meal we would be eating made my stomach do a slight roll, too. It turned out that night was every bit as wonderful as our first night in their home. We were lucky to have had that, but when we returned to our shanty the next day, we had to clean up a considerable amount of dirt that had coated everything.

Another dust storm raged just a few days later, and it seemed like dust storms would be a regular part of our lives in our new home. But by then, we had bought quite a few groceries, and we declined the kind invitation to eat with the Bridges family again and wait out another storm in their tightly built home. I was disappointed.

Our two-room shanty was anything but tight, and Mother made cloth masks and dampened them for us to wear while sleeping at night. The wind made whistling noises that sounded almost like a ghost howling, and it scared me. I knew about ghosts because one time when I was in first grade, my teacher had read a story to the class about a ghost, and she was very good at making ghost howls. But Daddy explained, "It's just the wind swirling through the loose wood siding on the outside of the shanty. Nothing to be afraid of."

The noises still frightened me when I was lying in my narrow bed in the corner of our dark kitchen. I pulled the sheet over my head so I would be less afraid of a ghost touching me. That turned out to be a better idea than I had realized. When I carefully peeled the sheet off my face the next morning, I noticed my mask had come off in the night, and the sheet was thickly coated with dust.

Still half-asleep, I walked barefoot across the gritty kitchen floor. My sleep had been interrupted too early by the harsh sounds of Mother clanking pans and dishes and her very unusual sputtering to herself: "Having to rewash the dishes and pans before I can make breakfast. Huh! I detest dust."

Her eyes were bloodshot and watery, and I understood why. Dust had sifted in through the walls and around the doors and windows. Perfect little pointed-top hills of dust sat on top of a layer of dust that blanketed the entire floor. The hills of dust reminded me of a picture I'd seen on a yellow-bordered magazine cover in a drugstore in Little Rock the time Grandpa and Grandma Dryden took us there in their nice car.

"Where's this place?" I had asked Mother, holding up the magazine. "Why're those squares of rock stacked up like hills with pointed tops? Did that funny-looking horse fall and break its back real bad?" I inquired.

"Oh, that's a picture of the pyramids in the Egyptian desert, where the ground is just sand with nothing green growing. The man's riding a camel, not a deformed horse," she answered.

That morning in the shanty, I decided I'd never go to Egypt, and not because camels live there, either. Who *would* like all that bare, dusty ground?

Dust—how terrible it is, I thought. I felt sorry for Mother. I could imagine how dusty the dishes and cooking utensils had become from sitting on open shelves instead of inside cabinets with doors. In the house back in Arkansas, Mother had gotten used to proper cabinets.

I could understand why she wouldn't see anything useful in dust, given the pain in her eyes, which was likely affecting her temperament. But in spite of my dislike for dust, I was tempted to draw a picture with my finger on the kitchen table's dust-coated oilcloth cover, but I suspected Mother would tap the back of my hand impatiently if she caught me doing it. So instead, with a short-handled brush called a whisk broom, I swept the dust off. Then I did my artwork on the oilcloth table cover in determined swipes with a damp cloth until it was dust free and shiny. Mother, in spite of her eyes blinking and watering, gave me a pleased look.

Pleasing Mother was important to me, most of the time anyway. Yes, I'd sometimes go out of my way to make her laugh, and I promptly did so that morning when I said, "At least we didn't get a big old centipede visitor last night."

~

There wasn't much difference between one dust storm and another that spring and early summer of 1933, and we pretty much did the same tasks to help each other endure them. For instance, while preparing a meal, we'd set the table and then cover the entire table with dish towels. When the food was cooked, Mother would stow the serving bowls of food under the towels until we were sitting at the table and she had prayed the blessing.

One morning after the dust storms had temporarily subsided, Daddy said, "Some folks are saying there's been thirty-nine dirty days this year. Others are saying there's been nearly fifty, counting from late January to the end of May." Then after telling Mother and me that bit of unofficial news, Daddy declared, "That would have been a dust storm nearly every other day. We dang sure had more good days than that."

The fact was, no one knew how many dust storms would be recorded for that year, but my father had put a positive spin on the weather conditions. He wanted us to have hope for the future, to believe there were better times ahead. I wanted to look forward to better times, too, and I was sure Mother did also. So in spite of the many dirty days, we viewed our living situation in the shanty as temporary, and we kept our eyes directed toward a brighter tomorrow.

Still, at least for Mother, there were times when Daddy's optimism and the exuberant graciousness of Mr. and Mrs. Bridges weren't quite enough to make up for the dust storms and the starkness of the land. On the other hand, at times during a clear day, both Mother and Daddy seemed awed by the unobstructed view of the vastness of the land in all four directions. Hundreds of acres of rain-needy wheat could be seen waving weakly in the wind, upstaging the stunted growth of small green fields in the slightly lower regions.

But even if neither of my parents had shown signs of appreciation for the beauty of our new location, I didn't expect us to ever turn back. For I remembered that at the end of our trip to Oklahoma my mother had said, "This journey was an investment in a dream," followed naturally by her gentle explanation of those words. I liked the idea that we had followed a dream, and I hoped it hadn't been a bad idea. Whenever I felt myself worry about a long trip back to Arkansas, I'd recall her words and feel better right away. But then I'd cross my fingers just in case.

~

As wheat harvesting time neared that summer, Daddy and Mr. Bridges talked about how the wheat a few miles northwest of us had totally fizzled due to the drought and dust storms. That sure sounded pretty bad, and I was worried at first, but then Mr. Bridges said, "My wheat crop is pitiful, but not that bad. The cotton's not much to crow about either, but we have to count our blessings, I guess."

While counting our own blessings one morning, Mother tried to project a little of her sense of humor with a wink and a nudge to my shoulder when she said, "Why, you even like your cot-size bed in the kitchen, don't you, Molly Girl?"

It always made me feel good when she called me Molly Girl, and I thought about her comment. She was right. I liked sleeping on my small bed in the kitchen. It was unique fun.

One of the kitchen windows was high up in the wall, and from my bed, I could see birds flying by at sunrise. I especially liked watching the rooster perched on the rooftop of the chicken coop. He'd shake his long, beautiful feathers, throw his head back, and crow as if he were the only grown-up male chicken in the world. One of those mornings I had asked Mother, "How come the rooster's so much prettier than the hens, and he crows like he's happy? When the hens lay an egg, they just cackle like they're upset."

"Oh, well, I guess that's God's will," was her response. But I didn't ask her to explain what she meant.

From my bed I could also see the windmill twirling round and round, pumping water from deep in the ground. I really enjoyed watching the windmill work as it pumped water for Mrs. Bridges's garden or into the tank for our drinking water. However, I must say, I didn't like the taste of that water.

I hadn't told my parents how much I disliked the strange-tasting water. We kept it in a wood bucket Daddy's Grandpa Dowden had given him as a housewarming gift when he and

Mother moved into the house in Arkansas. Some claimed a wood bucket kept water cooler than a bucket made of metal. I thought for sure it did.

One especially hot day, I stood in front of the kitchen window, my eyes on the water bucket, dreading to quench my thirst with the odd-tasting water. My thoughts floated back to an earlier time and place.

In my mind I could feel my heart leap in my chest as the water bucket materialized on the shelf of our Arkansas back porch. It was a pleasant porch shaded by the house and densely leafed, tall trees. I saw myself submerge the dipper into the bucket and bring it to my lips full of cool and pure-tasting water. I imagined savoring my sips while keeping my eyes on two mourning doves cooing softly as they strolled on the green moss covering the ground next to our porch.

But then suddenly—swoosh—two scissor-tailed flycatchers, southwest Oklahoma's most famous bird, zipped by our kitchen window and interrupted my reverie. They were on their way to perform their swooping and vaulting flight high above the barn, like the kites we'd seen one afternoon in a huge field not far from the farm.

I watched the birds' aerial antics for a while. But having been transported from my Arkansas fantasy back to the Oklahoma farm, I was still thirsty and dreading to drink the bitter-tasting water. *Gyp* water, folks called it. From listening to my parents' conversations, I figured out that gyp was a good label for the water. There were veins of gypsum mineral in the ground in a number of places, including nearby Thistleway, and these gypsum mineral veins tainted the taste of the water. I knew the lesson I needed to learn was *get used to it*. I also knew I'd better keep quiet about it.

~

A few days later, Mother and I were sitting in the shade of the shanty when Mr. Bridges brought Daddy home from Thistleway. Daddy walked briskly to where we sat with news to share with Mother: "Both Mr. Bridges and the president of Thistleway Bank, Ben Fleming, told me there's a surge of farmers leaving this area. And both of them said there would be a right-size farm available for us before long."

Daddy seemed as gleeful as a young boy. "Besides that," he said, "the mechanic at the gas station in Thistleway paid me a good deal more for the old truck than it would have cost me to have the engine fixed and to get new tires." Then with more happiness than I had noted for a while, he added, "The extra money will come in handy when we make a tenant farmer deal and when I buy a better truck."

I was pleased he had sold the old truck and thankful the jalopy hadn't conked completely while we were driving it to Oklahoma.

"I'm excited for you—yes, happy for us, Tillman," Mother said, "and Mrs. Bridges told me this morning that her husband would loan us a wagon with a team of horses so we can go to town anytime, or they'd loan us their truck if we should be in a hurry to get someplace."

"I know that, Elsa Ruth," snapped Daddy. "Mr. Bridges told me already. Don't you worry; we're going to be able to buy a good used truck later."

Daddy used Mother's middle name only when he was miffed at her or when he was teasing her. Mother nodded that she understood.

"Well, some of the well-off farmers are trading in their trucks that are still in very good condition for swanky new ones," Daddy continued in a softer tone. That relieved my mind, and I wondered what a swanky truck might look like. I also wondered if Mr. Bridges would be trading in his nice truck for a new one anytime soon.

~

My interest usually was stirred when Mrs. Bridges talked about the farm. She came to the chicken coop one day when I was inside handing the eggs out to Mother, and she told us Mr. Bridges had been planting a lot more wheat than cotton in recent years. "That's why we don't need two worker shanties anymore, except for a short time during cotton picking," she informed us. "Besides," she said more brightly, "grain crops could mean more money if the price goes up, and grain farming calls for a lot less labor than raising cattle, or for that matter, growing cotton. We hope, anyway."

Mother mentioned that Daddy hadn't given up hope on his dream of having milk cows and some beef stock on a farm with a large pasture.

"I hope it works out for him. I sure do," Mrs. Bridges said. But then she continued somberly, "Around the time of World War I, when the price of wheat was going up, a lot of farmers farther west of here plowed up their pastures and planted wheat instead of raising cattle. Some people say all that plowing up of the pasture grass is why we're getting dust storms. Grass roots really help to hold the dirt down, you know."

Mother looked concerned.

"You see, in dry spells," Mrs. Bridges explained, "there's not enough rain to grow the crops that keep the plowed soil solid so it won't blow away."

Mother sat openmouthed, holding her response until Mrs. Bridges finished before she said, "Land a mercy, I wish the farmers hadn't done that. But I guess they didn't know the damage it would cause."

I wondered why people, if they knew all that, were still planting crops that don't grow without rain instead of raising cattle. For if it made the dust storms worse, I just couldn't imagine that anyone would want to do that.

As Mrs. Bridges was leaving, she mentioned for about the third time since we had moved in that she was happy to have us on their farm.

"Sure hope you won't get tired of living in the cotton workers' shanty," she said as she patted Mother's hand.

"No," Mother said, "not at all." But I knew that was not quite true because we all wanted to live on our own farm as soon as possible.

I couldn't help feeling glad that one of the cotton pickers' shanties had been available for us. Even so, I worried a little that we'd still be living on this farm when it was time for school to start in the fall. I was hoping we would find our own farm long before then.

~

Before long we turned our calendar to July, and Mother marked my seventh birthday on the thirty-first. On that same day I heard Mother and Daddy discussing whether I would start the school year at the nearby country school or wait until we moved to our own farm.

"I think it's important Molly May doesn't have to switch schools," Daddy said emphatically.

"You're right," Mother answered. "She's shy around anyone except you and me. But she'll be all right with a little time. Remember how her first-grade teacher in Arkansas said she was an excellent student, in spite of being shy."

Another time I heard them referring to my lack of school clothes. Mother said, "I can make two of her outgrown dresses fit by sewing some solid-color strips of cloth on the sleeves and skirt bottoms."

Daddy didn't say anything.

"I might find the material on a remnant table for very little money," continued Mother. "Of course, I'd use only material that would match the main color in the dresses' print. It'll look nice."

I thought Daddy didn't seem to like the idea of the fixed-up dresses, and as soon as I could get a private moment with Mother, I asked her why Daddy didn't want her to make my old dresses fit me.

Mother explained, "Your daddy had a hard life when he was younger. When he was three, his mother died of breast cancer, as her mother did in her late thirties. His daddy was killed about two years later, when an untamed mule bucked him off and his head struck a large rock. So at age five or so, your daddy was an orphan, and as much as he wanted to, he couldn't stay with his Grandpa and Grandma Dowden except on weekends and a couple of weeks in the summer. You see, his grandpa said he was too old to be raising a young child—even though your daddy's dear grandmother strongly disagreed with him."

"That's strange," I interrupted. "Great-Grandpa Dowden didn't think he was too old when he married Maribelle, and he was a lot older then!"

My curious ears had always perked up at any mention of Daddy's youthful step-grandmother, Maribelle. I had figured out from listening to my folks talk a long time ago in Arkansas that she and Daddy's Grandpa Dowden had married not long after the accidental death of her twenty-five-year-old husband and the death of Daddy's beloved biological grandmother. While I wished I could have known my *real* great-grandmother, Maribelle's dresses were very spiffy. She was pretty and confident, and she was very sweet to me. I was glad Daddy's grandpa had married her. But from what I'd heard, he did not have the chance to enjoy being her husband for very long.

Unfortunately, soon after his death, mountain gossip said young Maribelle had married him more for his fine farm than for his seventy-plus-year-old charm. But Mother and Daddy paid little attention to such talk. They liked Maribelle, and they knew her deceased husband's folks had been wealthy people.

"Well, true enough! What you said about Grandpa Dowden's age when he married Maribelle," Mother said, finally responding to my comment. Then she added, "And I suspect he felt guilty in his later years because he hadn't taken your daddy in instead of putting him into foster care."

Foster care were scary words to me. "His foster parents weren't rich at all," Mother explained, "and your daddy had to wear hand-me-downs from the older children in his foster home. Some of the boys in school picked on him, and he figured they were treating him that way because his clothes were usually too small and he looked funny in them. Some of the tough mountain boys hid behind trees and big rocks and jumped out to pummel him when he was walking to and from school. But after your daddy finally bloodied a few noses, they left him alone."

Remembering how awkward I looked in my outgrown dresses, I could imagine how Daddy had felt. But I couldn't imagine how anyone—no matter how old or how tough they might be—could mistreat a child who didn't have a mother or a daddy.

~

A few days after Mother had filled me in on Daddy's sad childhood, he put on his newest-looking OshKosh overalls for town, and he and Mr. Bridges drove to Westin, about thirty miles away, to buy a tractor part. I couldn't help thinking my daddy sure liked to dress up when he could, because he felt he hadn't been able to as a child.

Daddy came back with a paper sack tucked under his arm. When he saw me eyeing the sack, he opened it and withdrew a piece of pink cloth and another piece in yellow, and said, "So your mother can fix up your two outgrown dresses."

Mother looked stunned, but she examined the material and said, "Sure looks like a color match to me. I should go get the dresses right now."

But before Mother could move, Daddy pulled my two old dresses from the bottom of the paper sack, laid them next to the material, and waited for her reaction.

I searched Mother's face for her approval, and what I saw was surprise; but she recovered quickly and cooed, "Oh, my goodness, you took the dresses with you? Why, just look—they *are* a good match!"

That was my father—at his best when we least expected it.

As he left the room, Mother and I bent our heads over the dresses and the perfectly matched material, and I heard her stifle a giggle before she said softly, "I guess your daddy is getting his mind ready to be the father of a second-grader."

The next morning, Mother quickly did her chores for Mrs.

Bridges and then finished her own work so she could begin the sewing project. For the next two days, she put in time mornings and evenings, sewing with the ancient foot-operated machine she had brought with her from Arkansas, and on the third day the dresses were finished, freshly laundered, and ready for school.

When I tried them on, I thought my legs looked as skinny as a newborn calf's, except I knew my legs weren't wobbly. Mother had told me more than once that, unlike a newborn calf, I could run as fast as lightning when I wanted to. Yet, I had to admit to myself that the dresses I'd seen on the cute, plump-legged girls in the old Sears catalog I brought with me from Arkansas looked different than mine. Prettier than mine. But then I told myself I was lucky—school would be starting soon, and I should feel proud in my fixed-up dresses.

But it turned out I wouldn't be wearing the dresses as soon as I had hoped. Mr. Bridges stopped by after supper with disappointing news.

"The country school won't be starting until maybe around November on account of an emergency in the young teacher's family, and the school board hasn't been able to find a substitute," he informed us.

"Not until maybe November, you say?" Daddy quickly questioned. Mr. Bridges shook his head and explained that the teacher's older sister in Texas was gravely ill and didn't have anyone to take care of her two small children. It was disappointing news for me, and it seemed my parents felt as I did.

~

Mrs. Bridges came by the next afternoon to see my school dresses, but she paid only scattered attention to me. Most of the time she spoke to Mother, confiding that she worried their cotton wasn't the best on account of infrequent and skimpy rains. I had heard over and over again that cotton badly needed rain to develop well, and I understood that the drought was on her mind. I tried hard to not be too disappointed that she barely looked at me as I pretended to model my altered dresses—for once not shy.

After Mrs. Bridges left, I put my dresses away, regretting I wouldn't be wearing them for a good while, and just as I expected, the weeks moved along at a snail's pace.

~

By October, the cotton bolls were cracking open, and white cotton was peeking out. The cotton pickers would soon move into the other workers' shanty just a little ways from ours, and I was excited. We hadn't grown cotton on the mountain, and I had never seen cotton harvested.

Both of the workers' places, the one we lived in and the one waiting for its seasonal occupants, were next to the cotton field. There was very little yard space on the other three sides of the two shanties. But that didn't matter much to me.

I seldom went outside, even when the heat let up. True, dust storm season was supposedly over, and after the heat of summer there were fewer whirlwinds, small but suffocating twisters of dirt that could sneak up on me. However, the sun was still quite hot, and there were no shade trees for me to play beneath, no grassy spots to romp on, and certainly no blossoming marigolds and mums to admire by the front door.

So, although I was curious and excited to see who would move into the other shanty, I figured I wouldn't see much of them, up close anyway. I wondered if I'd ever muster up the courage to amble across the yard with Mother to meet whoever would move in. I wished I could be as patient as Mother seemed to be about meeting our new neighbors. Once she teased, "You're spending an awful lot of time indoors with the children in your battered-up Sears catalog. I'm pretty sure you'll soon have live playmates right next door."

~

I figured both Mother and I were glad when the workers finally moved in. In fact, I almost forgot about my catalog friends and spent most of my time looking out our kitchen windows. I thought it was fun to watch the workers in the field.

Later, Mother explained, "Even though it's hot in the field, the workers have to wear long sleeves and gloves to protect them from the sharp burrs of the open cotton bolls." And when I asked why the women wore bonnets or cloths on their heads and the men wore straw hats, my eternal teacher answered, "To keep the hot sun off their heads, where the heat bothers most." That sounded reasonable to me, I thought, remembering how I always felt after going bareheaded in the sun for only a minute.

I could also see that all the workers were dark-faced people— darker than I had ever seen. But I was so happy to see other children, I didn't bother to ask Mother about the color of their skin. I counted two men and one woman, and several children, one boy about my age, one nearly grown, and several in between.

The workers snapped off the mature cotton bolls, exploding with white cotton, and stuffed them into their long sacks with wide shoulder straps that crossed their upper bodies. As they moved between two rows of cotton plants, snatching bolls from both sides, I could get a better look at their sacks. The children's sacks were not very long, but the adults' and the biggest teenagers' sacks were, and they looked like giant snakes slinking close behind them. I felt queasy thinking about snakes, and I quickly dismissed that image and instead listened to the workers sing, "Swing low, sweet chariot, coming for to carry me home," which caused me to ask Mother, "Is that a church song?"

"Yes, I think so. It probably was a song their great-grandparents sang a very long time ago, very likely while working in a cotton field, too," answered Mother.

My eyes scarcely wandered from the field as I watched them coming toward the end of the rows near our kitchen. Each worker would stop every few yards and vigorously shake the cotton toward the bottom of his or her sack. "Why're they shaking their sacks like that?" I asked Mother.

"Oh, they're trying to pack it down so they can get all of the cotton in the two rows they're working on into one sack," Mother answered.

When they finally had picked all of the ripe, fluffy cotton from the open bolls on both sides of their rows, they pulled their heavy sacks toward the high-sided wagon, where Daddy waited next to the scale to weigh each sack and record its weight in an orange-colored notebook. Then I'd see the workers climb into the wagon and pull their sacks up after them.

After they were standing in the wagon, they'd flap their long sacks up and down to force out rather high waves of white cotton, which looked to me like a flock of fluttering white birds escaping from some scary place. But what I liked best was still to come.

When their sacks were emptied and thrown to the ground, the workers seemed to be dancing on top of the cotton. I thought they needed a break from bending over so long in the field. But when I asked Mother why they were dancing, she said the cotton had to be packed down firmly so that when the wagon was full and taken to the cotton gin, it would weigh in heavy enough to make a bale. "What's a bale?" I wanted to know.

Glancing through the open kitchen door at something outside, she answered, "A bale is when the white, fluffy cotton is separated from the hard boll and the fluffy part is pressed until it's packed tight." Then, pointing toward the open door, she explained, "S-o-o, it'll be packed down, close to the size and shape of our toilet out there, and it'll be wrapped in a gunny-sack kind of material to hold it together. Well, anyway, it'll be a lot smaller than a wagonful."

All of that was interesting to me; it took the place of the pictures I would have enjoyed looking at or books I wished I could have been reading. And although I now knew the purpose of the dancing—stomping, or whatever it might be called—I still wanted to believe that packing down the cotton with their dance was a welcome relief from the backbreaking work in the field. They chattered and laughed while they were on top of the cotton, too, and that made me feel happy.

When the workers were at the far end of the field, I would take a few steps to the other window. From that window I had a good view of the younger children playing near their shanty. When they played a game of hopscotch, tag, or any other competitive game, I always wanted the girl to do better than the boys.

I'd heard them call her Charlene, which in my opinion was a very pretty name. I liked to say her name in my mind, and I couldn't help wishing I could play with her without feeling totally shy. I missed playing with the two friends I had back in Arkansas, and I thought it would be nice if Charlene could be my friend in Oklahoma.

~

One very sunny morning not long after the cotton pickers had moved in, Mother and I were walking along the end of the cotton rows on our way to the other shanty. When the workers glanced up at us, I could see them better because the sun shone brightly on their faces.

"How come those people are so dark?" I asked, pointing at the workers coming near the end of their rows.

"Oh, Molly Girl, sh-h-h, and don't point, and why didn't you ask me that when we were inside the house?"

I realized right away that I had asked something very sensitive, because Mother usually didn't react that sharply to my questions.

"Dark," she almost whispered, "is the natural color of their skin just like our light skin is our natural color. They're hardworking, good people just like us, though."

She looked around to see if anyone had heard, and I did, too. But the workers' backs were again bent in their labor.

"Mrs. Bridges told me there's two families, a woman named Myrtle and her sister."

Mother nodded.

"They're from a town called ..." I managed to say, pausing before I blurted, "well, maybe I didn't hear Mrs. Bridges right, because she held her hand over her mouth when she said 'Nigger Town, over in West End.'"

"Oh, good grief. You know it's Westin, not West End, and they're Negroes," Mother answered, hardly moving her lips. "And it's just plain not nice to call them or their section of town the name Mrs. Bridges called them. They live on the west side of Westin, and they can't get enough work there."

"How come they live there then?" I asked, feeling foolish I had misunderstood Mrs. Bridges.

Mother explained that their grandparents had moved from Tulsa to Westin in 1921 on account of the famous Tulsa Race Riots. "And that's just where their children and grandchildren have lived since then."

The words *race* and *riots* were hanging heavily in my mind, and even before Mother could begin to explain, I wanted to know their meanings. But Mother put her finger to her lips to signal another s-h-h-h.

"Let's not go into that right now," she answered. Then she quickly asked, "You remember the nice man from Tulsa we talked to when we stopped for gas right after we had crossed into Oklahoma? He bought you a bottle of grape soda pop, remember?"

I nodded after both questions, but what I remembered best was that I had feared the man might be Pretty Boy Floyd. He wore a suit and a hat, and he scared me when he ruffled my hair and said, "Want a bottle of pop, pretty-face girl?" I also remembered it was the first time I'd ever tasted any kind of pop.

As Mother and I continued our walk toward the workers' shanty, I suspected Mother's game had been to distract me from thinking about race and riots, because I was too young to know about such things. Although back then, even if you didn't know, you knew anyway. Right then I figured she probably wanted me to focus on our reason for going to our neighbors' shanty.

It was a very special occasion. Myrtle had given birth to twin baby boys in the shanty a few days before, and we were taking a very fine-looking three-layer frosted cake as a gift.

When we knocked at the screen door, I saw Charlene and her playmates skittering out the back door and a woman rushing toward us, her eyes popping open as big as chicken eggs. When she recognized us, she exclaimed, "Well, I do declare if ain't Miz Dowden and her girl chile. C'mon in, c'mon in and set down."

I suddenly went into one of my bashful spells, and I stepped a little behind Mother. While following close behind her hip, I peeked around and saw there were only two small wood chairs in the room and the rest of the space was filled with beds. I felt uneasy until Mother said, "Good morning. I'm Elsa Ruth, but just call me Elsa." Then Mother motioned me to step forward before she added, "And this is my daughter, Molly May. She and I made a cake for you on the occasion of your twins' birth. How you feeling? Myrtle, isn't it?"

"Myrtle it is, and I'm fine and dandy, Miz Elsa," she answered while taking the cake and sniffing its spicy aroma. "This cake sure do smell good. Now I'm puttin' this fine cake where the dog won't come sniffing around it. Thank you, thank you. Y'all is the nicest folks."

Mother assured her we were pleased to bring the cake and to have a chance to get acquainted. Myrtle smiled.

Finally, Mother asked Myrtle the question I'd been waiting for her to ask. "And are you showing off those fine twin boys of yours yet?"

"Sure nuff," Myrtle quipped as she set the cake on a high shelf. Then she beckoned us to follow her to the kitchen, where she led us between more beds. At the same time, she looked over her shoulder at us and said, "This awful nice. I never had a white lady come calling afore."

She led us to the corner of the kitchen where the babies were. I peeked at the tiny babies sleeping in a cardboard box with a regular bed-size quilt folded several times so that it made a thick mattress beneath them. The infants were curled tightly together like two spoons lying sideways in a drawer. As my peek became a gaze, I had a foolish thought, for a seven-year-old: *Since these babies are exactly alike, maybe Myrtle will tell me I can take one home with me for a little while so I can pretend it's my doll.* But I stepped down on my silly thought quickly, and another thought came to me.

"What're their names?" I asked, surprised at my sudden burst of boldness, but I was instantly pleased to learn they were called Al and Bert, after their grandfather Albert.

As much as I had enjoyed the visit, as we were leaving I still couldn't pull up enough confidence in myself to tell Myrtle the babies were cute. But Mother thanked her for letting us see her babies, and she gave her several compliments on them.

~

"I wish Myrtle coulda give me one of the babies for a little while," I whispered as I was supposed to, when Mother and I were walking back to our shanty.

"*Could have given, could have given*, Molly Girl," Mother corrected me, and it seemed to me that after I had turned seven she had been correcting the way I talked a lot. "And," she continued, "having two babies and not being able to tell one from the other doesn't mean she could, or should, loan out one. No, that's not a way to share."

I thought to myself that we had just shared our cake with the two families, even though we hardly ever had cake since moving into the shanty. I liked cake very much and could eat it every day.

Actually, I had understood sharing all along. Once, while I was watching Charlene play outside with the boys, I'd thought about sharing one of my brand-new pencils with her, if we ever should play together. Mr. Bridges had given me the bright blue pencils, with "Thistleway Cotton Gin" printed on them in gold, and they were very special to me.

But I concluded I needed to think for a while before letting one of my pencils out of my hands. I eased my guilt over not sharing by imagining the cotton gin giving pretty pencils like mine to farmers every time they brought a wagonload of cotton to the gin. Then I pictured Mr. Bridges giving Charlene a couple.

~

Mother and I returned to the good people's shanty twice during their stay so that I could see the twins, but the other children always scooted out the other door as soon as we knocked. So I never had a chance to play with them. Mother often waved to Myrtle and the others or exchanged greetings with them from across the yard, and I felt like doing the same, but I didn't. I let Mother's social skills represent mine, too, and I was sure I'd miss seeing the children after their return to Westin. That day came all too soon.

~

After the workers moved, I trooped across one morning to the vacant shanty while Mother and Mrs. Bridges were picking squash, which they would be canning all day. They'd be head-to-head talking and wouldn't miss me until lunchtime, I hoped.

My heart pounded hard and fast as I looked about the two rooms, but not so much because I felt like a trespasser, but because of my gnawing fantasy. I imagined that one of the babies had been unintentionally left behind. But deep down I knew that was babyish of me, and I soon focused my hopes on finding an empty baby talcum can, a baby sock, or the tin can the children had kicked around outside. I thought anything that would remind me of the babies and the children who had lived and played there would be special.

I didn't find a keepsake, but I had a feeling I'd never forget them.

~

Two days later, we learned my teacher had returned from Texas, and school would open the following Monday. I could hardly wait.

The next day, it was very pleasant, and Mother coaxed me into going outside to play and get some fresh air.

I wandered over to the empty workers' shanty. But I didn't want to go inside. *Too quiet, too lonely in there*, I thought to myself, still regretting that the children and I hadn't been able to overcome our reluctance to play together.

Instead of entering the shanty, I sauntered around to the shade in back where I had often seen the children rest from their play in the hot sun. Then, noticing a narrow stack of firewood about waist-high piled against the shanty, I climbed to the top of the stack and jumped off. Flying through the air when I jumped off the woodpile felt good, and I did it over and over until my hair and the top part of my dress felt wet with sweat.

Finally, I sat down on the top of the woodpile, leaned the back of my head against the side of the shanty, and feasted my eyes on the cloudless blue sky. I stretched my arms out on both sides of the woodpile and let them hang limply. Suddenly I became aware that my fingers on my right hand were touching something strangely sticky, and then I felt a stinging pain on the top of my hand.

I jerked my hand away from the wood and looked down to see if a wood splinter had caused the pain. There was no splinter, but I saw what was left of a spiderweb with a shiny black spider clinging to it.

Like a startled rabbit, I jumped off the woodpile and ran to Mother, who was already coming to check on me. When I told her about the spider and my painful hand, she quickly picked me up and raced to the woodpile. When she saw the spider, her expression turned grim and she said, "It's a black widow. I can see the red hourglass mark on her belly."

I knew it was not the time for asking what an hourglass was, but I did ask if a black widow bite was a bad thing. Mother only said, "Mrs. Bridges told me about them. Let's go find her."

My hand hurt as much as it had one time before we moved to Oklahoma when I had a long splinter of wood under my fingernail. But I had no knowledge of how serious a black widow bite might be, and I certainly had no idea what the next few weeks would be like for my parents and me.

When Mrs. Bridges opened her door, her eyes instantly fastened on Mother, and with a worried look on her face, she asked, "Has something gone wrong, Elsa? You look pale."

But when she heard a black widow had bitten me, she turned her attention to me. As soon as she saw the two tiny puncture marks on my hand, she said, "Thank the good Lord we have an icebox. Sit right down, and I'll make an ice pack to put on that bite. You'll need to keep the ice on the bite for a good while."

After a while I felt nauseated, and Mrs. Bridges rushed to get a bucket for me to vomit into. After that, I whimpered, "I feel like lying down." And Mrs. Bridges and Mother each took one of my arms to help me up from the chair. They managed to get me on my feet, but my legs wouldn't hold me up, and I would have fallen down had they not held me. And they more or less dragged me to the bed where I had slept so peacefully when we were newcomers.

After they tucked me into bed, Mrs. Bridges straightened her back and said, "I'll ring the big dinner bell hanging on the porch to signal the men to come from their fence mending, but I don't know if they'll hear it over on the far side of our land where they're working today. Oh, and I'll call the doctor."

It turned out the doctor's wife told Mrs. Bridges on the phone that her husband was delivering a baby about fifteen miles away. Besides that, she didn't know of anyone in that area who had a phone so she could contact him. All she could suggest was that I should have the ice pack on the bite marks for twenty minutes at one-hour intervals, and I should be given plenty of fluids and one aspirin with a little milk and bread when the pain became severe.

By the time Mr. Bridges and Daddy came in at dusk from their fence mending, the site around the spider bite was turning purplish blue. Pain was permeating through my arms, legs, and stomach. Later, cold sweat covered my entire body. I shivered, and my legs went from painful to unbearable cramping. And from far away I heard Daddy saying, "Her eyelids are swelling up," and Mr. Bridges telling him soothingly that I'd be all right.

But my mind weakly replayed only Daddy's remark, and I vaguely wondered if my eyelids would keep swelling until they burst like a balloon. What a dud I'd be in school, more shy than ever without eyelids. I closed my eyes just to appreciate the fact that I still could, and I must have fallen asleep.

When I awoke, I heard Mr. Bridges asking Mother questions about where I was when the spider bit me. I could barely see him, but I had a sense that he examined the two tiny spider bite holes on my hand; then more clearly, I heard him say, "It's late in the year for a widow to bite, but if Molly May disturbed her web, she'd been apt to bite, all right." I wanted to tell him I sure hadn't meant to disturb anything.

~

One day ran into the next, and although I barely remembered the talk around me, I remembered the doctor at my bedside telling my folks I'd probably not have much of an appetite for a few days, but to make sure I ate anyway. I also remembered how unpleasant the fluids and pureed foods had been and that I feared I'd never again be able to eat solid foods. When I was finally well enough, Daddy carried me to our place, where I languished for several more days. I still ate very little and lost more weight and strength.

Although my appetite finally returned, along with some increased weight and strength, I still tired easily. The doctor assured my folks that all my symptoms were normal and that tiring easily was just one of them. Nonetheless, my folks decided I should not begin school until after Christmas. Of course, Mother taught me at home in half-hour sessions, three times a day, and I practiced my acquired reading comprehension skills on the backs of used envelopes and wrapping paper Mother and Mrs. Bridges had saved for me.

It was obvious reading and then writing my answers to questions about the stories Mother had written for me was my favorite activity, but I was a long way from enjoying my work with numbers. But Mother soon nudged up my level of proficiency in addition and subtraction well enough for me to recognize there might be some excitement in learning arithmetic, and again the reusable paper came in very handy when I did the practice problems.

Daddy picked up a U.S. road map at the gas station so Mother could teach me some geography. Before long she had me drawing my own maps on the backs of old letters.

Considering I was Mother's only student, she tried to make my temporary schooling at home as real as possible. She had passed the teacher certification exam after finishing eleventh grade, but Daddy wanted to get married. In those days, schools in some areas didn't want to hire married women. I was sorry my mother had to give up her plans to be a teacher. That was why I wanted to prove to Mother that she would have been a very good one, had she been given the chance.

Mother encouraged me to write all of the new words I'd recently learned from reading the little stories she had written for me. I wrote the new words on the first page of a journal Grandma Dryden had sent me for my seventh birthday. On the day it arrived, I had printed at the very top of the first page, "Molly May Dowden Starts Second Grade 1933." I did it all very carefully, and it reminded me of a real book, and I was eager to be older so I could write very good stories in it, too. I thought one of my stories should be about our first dust storm experience, and it would include the episode about the centipede biting the frail boy. I asked Mother how to spell centipede, and I wrote the word on the second page of my journal as a reminder to someday write the story.

~

I sure didn't want for education, but I *did* want us to get our own farm. I overheard a lot of talk about Daddy's progress in finding one. Mr. Fleming at the bank sent him letters from time to time or called Mr. Bridges asking him to relay information concerning farms in foreclosure. But crop prices had almost hit bottom, and the available larger farms that had been converted to grain farming would require expensive oversized farm equipment like tractors, heavy-duty cultivators, and plows. Without the money to purchase big machinery, Daddy had few choices.

I was worried we'd never find our own place.

At night when the work was done, my folks' hope about finding the right farm seemed to grow stronger, and somehow it weakened in equal amounts in the light of day. By early November something strange was happening to me, too. The lingering fatigue from the spider bite was one thing, but on top of that I often felt sad. That troubled me. I wanted to be strong and happy.

I no longer appreciated the rustic sounds of the rooster's early morning crowing, the hens' cackling, or the windmill's faint, rhythmical squeaking throughout the day. I vaguely wondered if I'd feel better if there were a tree with a sturdy branch on which Daddy could put a swing. I could swing on a warm November afternoon, I mused. But soon my desire to imagine these things faded. My optimism about living somewhere other than the workers' shanty diminished as well. Only my lessons with Mother made the long, seemingly gray days tolerable.

Other than my parents' voices, there were very few voices in my life, and none of them belonged to other children. We didn't have a phone or radio in our house, so no one ever called to say 'hi,' and music never came over the airwaves. It was a quiet, lonely house. And to me it was drab, too. I was sure that not even beautiful things like Mrs. Bridges's possessions would make it any brighter or happier. And the sadness stayed with me. Even the thought of Christmas next month didn't cheer me up. There was, however, one event every morning that held my attention, for the few minutes that it lasted: watching Daddy shave at the kitchen mirror.

His ivory-handle, straight-edge razor, with its long, shimmering blade, had been a birthday gift from his beloved Grandma Dowden not long before her death. And although I had never had a chance to see the razor up close, it was special in my mind.

One morning after Mother had eaten her breakfast quicker than usual and Daddy had wolfed down his biscuits and two of the eggs Mr. Bridges had brought us, I lingered at the table nibbling my biscuit and molasses while watching Daddy's face in the mirror.

He shaved shirtless at the wash basin, which sat on a shelf beneath the mirror. His brow and his eyes appeared worried while he shaved hurriedly—and I recalled the reason why. Mr. Bridges was taking him to see Mr. Fleming at the bank to talk about a farm that would soon be available.

When Daddy had finished, he put his shaving mug and lathering brush on the shelf above the mirror, and I noticed he hadn't put away his razor. But I assumed he'd put it in its proper place after he finished splashing water on his face to remove the remaining streaks of white shaving lather. And I went back to feeling sad.

As soon as Daddy had rushed to the bedroom and put on his shirt and shoes, he ran out the kitchen door, leaving it wide open. The house became quiet. I considered going outside to help Mother tend the chickens, but she, too, had seemed to be in a big hurry when she left, and I thought it best not to tag along. I thought I'd just slow her down.

I soon heard Mr. Bridges's truck engine putt-putting outside our kitchen door and Mother from a distance calling, "'Bye, Mr. Bridges. 'Bye, Tillman. I hope it goes well today."

I hope? I hadn't heard those words for several days. Maybe things would be different today. Perhaps Daddy would come home with good news. And I hoped *that* would get me out of my doldrums.

～

As the sound of the truck's engine faded into the distance, I felt my hope take another dip. But instead of giving in to it, I stood up and said out loud to myself, "It's time for me to stop dilly-dallying and do something useful." That was what I had heard Mother say after taking a rest once in a rare while. I felt like I was finally in gear and ready to roll.

The kitchen door was open, reminding me that Daddy's shaving water was still sitting with globs of his beard-speckled shaving lather floating on its surface. It needed to be dashed outside onto the thirsty ground where he always threw it. But just as I was about to pick up the wash basin, I noticed the razor still lying partially open. I knew Daddy simply wasn't that careless with his razor. He always placed it on the shelf above the mirror, along with his shaving mug and brush. Right away, my seven-year-old logic told me I needed to take action.

Quickly, I pushed a kitchen chair across the room so I could stand on it to reach the shelf above the mirror. What happened next seems like a very bad dream whenever I recall it.

～

After closing the razor, I held it in my left hand and hoisted myself to a standing position on the seat of the chair. A few seconds later, the chair jiggled as I tried to reach the shelf where the shaving mug and brush were stored. I almost dropped the razor, but caught it instead by slamming it against my hip. But before I could breathe a sigh of relief, I felt a sudden burning pain across my palm. That confused me. I had closed the razor before I climbed up on the chair. I wondered if my fingers had been a little sticky and had somehow caused the razor to open. But that didn't seem reasonable. Or maybe I just imagined the pain. I looked down, and clearly, brilliant red polka dots and stripes were appearing down the front of my dress, and on my bare feet, the chair, and the floor.

Right away, Daddy's emphatic words when I was younger romped back into my brain: "Now look here, Molly May, don't ever mess with this here razor—for it will hurt you real bad." Then he said barely loud enough to be heard, "Little girls can be awful nosy sometimes."

Almost paralyzed for a moment with Daddy's words still bouncing around inside my head, along with guilt and panic canceling out my desire to be helpful, I let the razor fall to the floor, and I howled, "Mother-r-r-r."

Before I could have said scat, Mother dashed through the doorway, her eyes flashing from me to the open razor on the floor, and back to me.

"Aw-w-w, Molly Girl, you shouldn't have touched your daddy's old shaver!" was all she said.

In only about two ticks of the clock, she lifted me from the chair and gave my face a brief stroke. Then darting from one task to the next as fast as a streak of lightning, she tore strips from a clean dish towel, put a tourniquet around my wrist, folded a thick compress for the cut across my palm, and wrapped the remaining wide strip of towel snugly around my hand. Then she stood to her full height and said quietly, "We'll go to the doctor. He can fix it."

I recalled Mrs. Bridges had gone on a train to visit her daughter in Oklahoma City, and Daddy and Mr. Bridges were in Thistleway. That meant we had no way of getting to the doctor quickly. But before I could even begin to worry, Mother squatted and commanded me to get on her back. So with my legs wrapped around her waist and her arms firmly hooked around both of my legs, I rode on her back, clinging to her shoulder with my uninjured hand to steady myself. *Where is she taking me?* I wondered.

Only a few steps later Mother said, "It won't be too bad a run across the pasture to the Bradshaws'. They own a car and can take us to the doctor."

But the going wasn't exactly clear sailing. At times Mother had to skirt around patches of thick prickly pear or gourd vines, sprawling wide and green on the ground as though there was no drought at all. Twice she had to give a wide path to a snake coiled on gyp rock basking in the late autumn sun. Finally, there was a fuzzy black tarantula that seemed about as big as my hand, with legs as long as my fingers, commanding us to take a detour.

All of that troubled me, and I also worried that no one would be home at the Bradshaw place once we got there. When I asked Mother if she was sure Mr. Bradshaw would take us to the doctor, she replied, "I know he'll take us to the doctor, unless he's sitting at a baseball game like your daddy does every day." Then panting for breath, she glanced over her shoulder at me, grinned, and said, "I'm trying to be funny, honey."

It was a line I'd heard Daddy say to her when she hadn't seemed to appreciate his humor, and so I tried to lighten up.

As we were nearing the Bradshaw place, I noticed Mother was breathing harder, and I wanted her to allow me to run beside her. But at the same time something alarming a few yards to our left caught my eye, and I asked, "Is that Mr. Bradshaw's mean old bull Daddy told us about?"

She took a quick glance and said, "Oh-h, bless my soul, yes!" Then she whispered, "Let's pray, starting right now. Whisper, so the bull can't hear us."

It hadn't helped that I had always let Mother do the praying at night when we knelt by my narrow bed in the corner of the kitchen. In my mind I had thanked God for some things. But I had never asked him for any favors—not even a doll for Christmas—on account of being shy as heck about talking to any "him," especially one I couldn't see. But soon I could feel the bull getting close to my back, and I whispered, "Please, God, let Mother outrun this mean old bull."

We made it through the gate near the Bradshaws' big white house. After Mother had locked the gate against the bull, she helped me slide down from her back. Then we both looked back and saw that the bull was still grazing where we had first seen him.

Mother and I looked at each other with little half smiles of embarrassment before she let out her breath with, "Whew!"

Then, with our perils behind us, we focused our attention on the Bradshaw house. Just before we reached the front door, we spotted Mr. Bradshaw leaving his barn. At the same time, he saw us and rushed forward in spite of his limp. He quickly realized we needed a doctor, and he said, "Dr. Winfrey is a partly retired doctor. He has an office in his home now, and he lives this side of Thistleway. I went to him when I broke my leg, and he did a good job on it."

Mother immediately favored his suggestion, and she said, "Yes, I know. He's our doctor, too."

Mr. Bradshaw helped us into his fine-looking car, with both a front and a back seat. Daddy had said more than once that the car was a well-cared-for beauty, and it was. As I settled into the roomy back seat, I noticed his truck by the barn and marveled at someone who could own two vehicles at the same time.

When Mother loosened the tourniquet on my hand to let the circulation flow for a little while, I worried the swell car would be soiled. But Mr. Bradshaw didn't seem concerned about his car. He just glanced over his shoulder at me and said, "You should come and play sometime with my daughter. She's only two years older than you."

I didn't think that was a very good idea. I'd never even seen his daughter, and she wasn't my age. But I thought Mr. Bradshaw was very nice. He was a good bit older than Daddy, and I wagered to myself that he drove faster than he had ever driven in his life, even to a house fire or a barn fire. We were sitting in the doctor's office in no time.

All the while the elderly doctor cleaned my hand for surgery, he mumbled about cases he'd had in which there had been careless parents and injured children. But before long, Mother firmly interjected, "Doctor, my husband's not careless; this morning there were unusual circumstances."

The doctor only glanced at Mother when she said that, and when he had finished stitching and bandaging my hand, he turned to her and said, "That will be fifty cents."

I didn't know if fifty cents was more or less than Mother had expected, but I did know the look on her face was not one I'd seen before.

"Doctor," Mother responded, "I sure don't like to ask, but

could you take three dozen of my homemade sugar cookies for payment, or if that's not enough, I could also do some mending for you."

After a pause he answered, "Well, all right, drop off the cookies the next time you're going by, and never mind about the mending." And then he added, "Um-m, you did a good emergency treatment on your daughter, Mrs. Dowden, but you shouldn't have carried a seven-year-old child across that pasture. I know she's a thin child, but you still shouldn't have."

Dr. Winfrey's words made me ashamed of myself for causing Mother to do something that she shouldn't. But I reminded myself that she had carried me on her back a couple of times back in the summer when I was running and forgot that I was barefoot and stepped into a patch of goathead stickers.

"The stickers hurt so much, especially if one breaks off into the bottom of your foot. Try to remember not to step into a patch of them," Mother would say while picking the stickers from the bottoms of my bare feet.

Later, as we were leaving the doctor's office, I noticed Mother walked a little bent over and held her hand on her back. She normally was a strong-looking, straight-standing woman, and I didn't like seeing her any other way.

~

The next morning, Mr. Bridges knocked at our kitchen door before daybreak. I couldn't make out much of what was said except that Mr. Bridges was driving over to Westin right away to pick up his missus at the train station, and that he had telephoned Mrs. Bradshaw about some matter or other. What it was I couldn't hear at all.

My folks had woken me and fed me breakfast way before daylight, and I was too tired to strain much to hear Mr. Bridges. I was deep in my own thoughts anyway; I was quite sure it was my fault that Mother's back was still hurting. Right after breakfast, she had said she was going back to bed to rest a little. I had seen from the kitchen doorway that Daddy sat on the edge of the bed next to her, and I was left to stew in my own juice of worry and guilt.

Something else was on my mind, too. At breakfast Mother and Daddy had told me that later in the morning I was going to the Bradshaws' house to play with their daughter. Mother had looked me in the eye and said, "Mrs. Bradshaw wants you to come real bad. It's Saturday, and her daughter won't be in school. It's a good chance for you to play with a child pretty close to your age. She's only nine."

Maybe I didn't want to play with the girl because I was worried about Mother. Or maybe it was because the razor incident had occurred only the day before. Or maybe I would have liked to see how she seemed with other children, especially children my age, before I was forced to play with her. Or maybe I was just very tired. Yet one thing was for sure: I didn't want to play with the Bradshaw girl, not that day, anyway. But something in Daddy's eyes told me to go along with it. I knew I'd better mind my step, or he would remember he hadn't given me an angry scolding for messing with his razor.

Not long after Mr. Bridges left, Daddy wrapped me in a blanket, as it was much colder than the day before, and took me out to the wagon with the horses already hooked up to it—thanks to Mr. Bridges, I imagined. Daddy plunked me onto the wagon seat and climbed up beside me. As we rode along in the crisp morning air, I kept thinking about having to go to a strange house to play with a girl I'd never seen before. Yet I knew I shouldn't ask questions, because Daddy might not have much patience. After all, he was taking me to the Bradshaws' house when he needed to be milking Mr. Bridges's cows. There was always something to worry about, things bigger than myself, and I knew that. So I stayed quiet.

~

When we arrived at the Bradshaws', Daddy thanked Mrs. Bradshaw for inviting me, and then he left me standing inside the front entry of the big white house.

Finally managing to take a few steps into what they called the parlor, I realized I was in a home even larger and prettier than the home of Mr. and Mrs. Bridges. Worse, I was face-to-face with a girl who was two years older—and dressed in pretty clothes. That was more than a little bit scary. But ready or not, there I was, hardly able to do more than glance at my nine-year-old hostess or her mother, both of them hovering near the other doorway of their fancy parlor.

"Hello, my name is Helen Marie," the girl said, and then gesturing toward her mother, she added, "and this here's my mother. You can call her Mrs. Bradshaw."

"'Lo, miss; 'Lo, ma'am," was all the social poise I could muster before my eyes were scanning the nice furnishings once again.

After what seemed like a very long silence, Mrs. Bradshaw asked sweetly if my hand was feeling better.

I nodded and allowed my heavily bandaged hand to glide— unnoticed, I hoped—from my waist to behind my hip.

"Well," spoke Mrs. Bradshaw, changing to a citified voice, "it looks like our young visitor needs a little time to get used to us."

I was very glad she had said that, but I reckoned the situation was going to take a lot of getting used to. Helen Marie was pretty as a picture with her golden hair styled in curls and dressed in a bright floral print dress, shiny shoes, and all. She looked like she had marched right out of my Sears catalog. Her manners and clothes were making me aware of my lack of nice ways, dull-colored dress, dusty shoes, and dark blond, straight-as-a-stick hair. "Buster Brown style," Daddy always claimed, while giving me my monthly haircut.

"When's my daddy coming back?" I asked, suddenly missing my home, embarrassed because I sounded more urgent than I intended.

"Oh, I think about suppertime," answered Mrs. Bradshaw cheerily.

I was glad I'd had the good sense to look at her while she answered me, but then my mental comparisons intruded again. She, too, looked like she was from a catalog page, in her pretty print dress and color-matched, perky apron. With her very short hair she looked exactly like the women in my catalog.

From seeing pictures, I knew Mother's pretty red hair had been cut stylishly short at one time, but after we moved to Oklahoma, she had let it grow long and combed it straight back and twisted it into a bun pinned at the nape of her neck. "Prairie style," she called it. Her plain dress was drab-colored, coarse cotton, and she often wore a dish towel tied around her middle for an apron.

The attention on me finally let up a bit, and Helen Marie showed me her piano and told me she was taking lessons. To have a piano *and lessons* was unimaginable to me! She invited me to read one of her books or play with her many toys, but I touched them only with the fingertips of my good hand. I had to admit to myself the girl was nice, but I still needed to see her with other children away from her home before I could be sure she would be a good friend for me.

Soon Mr. Bradshaw came in from his work, and Mrs. Bradshaw invited us to the kitchen for a snack of peanut butter and bakery-made white bread sandwiches and fresh, red apples.

I had never tasted peanut butter. My sandwiches at home were usually made with leftover breakfast biscuits and cold side pork, or if I was lucky, some pieces left over from a chunk of home-cured ham that Mr. Bridges sometimes gave us.

As I sat at the Bradshaws' table, I recalled that the only taste of apple I'd had since we arrived in Oklahoma had been a few slices of dried apple I'd begged from Mother when she was making fried apple fritters for the Fourth of July. The fritters were delicious with the homemade ice cream Mrs. Bridges gave us on that special holiday. Recalling that day, I tried to convince myself those treats were as special as bakery-made bread and fresh apple.

Strangely, I don't remember Daddy's picking me up at the Bradshaw house or anything about the ride home in the wagon. What stuck in my mind occurred right after we returned home.

Daddy ushered me through our kitchen to his and Mother's bedroom. I was shocked, and then frightened, by what I saw and heard. Mother was lying in bed, with long sprigs of her red hair sticking to her face and pillow. Her normally creamy complexion looked as colorless as Grandma Dryden's everyday dishes. I stopped and stood, confused until she motioned for me to come toward her, and in a strangely soft voice she said, "Come on over here, Molly Girl."

Fear spread over me just like it had lately when I thought about black widow spiders and what their bites could do to you.

For I imagined she would be lying in bed looking pale and sounding weak for a long time, maybe forever. But then I noticed a baby at her side struggling to nurse just like I'd once seen a newborn calf do with its mother.

"Look what the doctor brought while you were playing at the Bradshaws' house," Mother offered with subdued delight.

"It's little Lettie Ruth, your very own baby sister, as pretty and sound as a little rock. Even if she did come a month early," Daddy announced proudly.

~

My baby sister enthralled me with every sound and movement she made, but I kept a low profile around Daddy because I feared he would recall he still hadn't punished me for messing with his razor. But at breakfast about a week after my sister was born, Daddy looked across the table at me and said, "I'm not mad at you about the razor. I guess you were just trying to help." After a pause he added, "You'll never touch it again. Isn't that right?"

"I won't, Daddy," I said.

Later, I asked Mother if she thought Daddy was mad at me for all the trouble I'd caused with the razor.

"Why, no, Molly May!" Mother exclaimed. "He told me he blamed himself for forgetting to put the razor away. He was angry only because we couldn't afford to buy toys for you so that you wouldn't have to look for something to do that might hurt you. He thought you were just a curious little girl, and lonely."

Mother's reassurance was what I needed, and I set aside my memory of Daddy's words "little girls can be nosy," and let Mother's good confirmation of Daddy's feelings encourage me to ask her a question I'd wanted to ask since I had first laid eyes on my baby sister: "Why wasn't I let in on the secret, about a baby coming?"

"Well, for one thing, we thought you might notice a baby was coming, because my stomach was getting big, and if you had asked, we would have told you right then. Besides that, your daddy and I were concerned about a lot of things, and we kept putting off our decision about when would be the right time to tell you," she answered.

I nodded that I understood, except I wondered why she'd think I'd notice my own mother's stomach getting big just because she had told me one time what was happening when I noticed a cow's stomach getting bigger. No, I hadn't noticed Mother's growing stomach, because it was like hair getting longer. Some things happen so gradually you just don't see them until someone calls your attention to it.

"Not only that," Mother said, while lifting Lettie Ruth from her bed, "we were worried Mr. Bridges wouldn't get back from picking up Mrs. Bridges at the train station in time for one of them to use their phone to call the doctor to come deliver the baby. We also figured your hand was hurting too much for it to be the right time to tell you."

She said all that while walking to where I sat. Then she carefully placed my precious baby sister in my arms.

"That makes sense to me," I said, mimicking words I'd heard Mother say often, while I gently stroked my sister's soft, pale brown hair with my uninjured hand. "And you know what else?" I continued as I looked up at Mother. "I love my baby sister with all my heart. She's brought beauty into our house. She's our Christmas gift."

"Speaking of Christmas gifts …" Mother responded as she took a box from a shelf and extended it toward me.

"What's this?" I asked.

"It's an early Christmas gift. Open it, honey child. Here, I have two hands. Let me hold the baby while you open it."

Mother had already taken off the outer wrapping paper, and all I had to do was slip the cover off the box. Inside was a beautiful little summer dress for Lettie Ruth that she would wear several months later and a pair of knee-high socks for me, both gifts from Maribelle.

"How did Maribelle know so soon about our baby?" I asked.

"Well, the day our baby was born Mrs. Bridges called Grandpa and Grandma Dryden to tell them," answered Mother, "and I guess they must have told Maribelle. They sometimes see her in church."

~

Lettie Ruth couldn't have been a more pleasant baby. In addition to our happiness about having her with us, we made the best of our Christmas Day and opened a card from Grandpa and Grandma Dryden with two one-dollar bills in it. Otherwise, Christmas seemed to slip by that year with little fanfare. In retrospect I'm not surprised. Having a new baby overshadows everything.

Chapter Three

Christmas Day had fallen on a Sunday, and the day after Christmas we learned that banker Ben Fleming had called Mr. Bridges and told him the farm they had discussed on the day of the razor incident was now available and that it might work for us. It was five miles southeast of Thistleway, while the farm where we currently lived was ten miles west. In my mind, that was too far away from Mr. and Mrs. Bridges, the folks who had become my stand-in grandparents. But 1934 would be rolling in within a few days, and a new year lay ahead of us.

As soon as Mrs. Bridges learned about the prospect of our getting a farm of our own, she offered to take care of Lettie Ruth while we went to look at it. Mr. Bridges insisted we use their truck.

~

Two days after Christmas, we went to see the farm. While he drove us there, Daddy, who had seen the farm right before Christmas, made it clear that the important thing for Mother to realize about the farm was that he liked its fairly good soil and the "lay of the land," as he called it. He pointed out that there were plenty of rabbits on its large pastureland and that he could hunt them so we'd have more meat on our table. He explained that the pasture had long, narrow gullies that would hold water for several days after a rain and would nourish thick grass along the gullies' banks. "That'll be a feast for the cows when the rest of the pasture grass gets scarce," he boasted.

On our arrival at the farm, Daddy hurried off to inspect the land again, and Mother at first only peeked inside the house, crinkled her nose, and turned back toward the truck. I was afraid to enter the house alone, but a moment later she returned, and we stepped inside the house together. She cast a displeased look about its three rooms as we walked through them and quickly exited through the back door muttering, "Good enough for chickens." I tagged along behind her.

~

Daddy returned to the house excited after a better look at the fenced outlet that would give our livestock access to water from a narrow creek that bordered the farm. "Teal Creek, I'll call it because I saw two Teal ducks swimming in its waters," Daddy exclaimed while his face beamed. "It's got some trees along its bank, and I think maybe with some squirrels in them. It's a shallow, pebbly, and rock-bottom creek that curves around for several yards next to our farm. And there's grass on its bank for the cows."

"All of that's good to know, Tillman, but what about drinking water?" Mother responded in a monotone voice, which made it clear even to me that she wasn't thrilled with this particular farm.

Ignoring her seeming disinterest, Daddy quickly asked her to go with him to check out the old cistern next to the back door.

The gutter system along the roof was fine and channeled the rainwater into the cistern, just as it was supposed to do. But they were disappointed when they found cracks in the cistern's concrete not very far from ground level. Cracks in the wall of the cistern meant the water would not be safe to drink, and that meant there was no potable water on this farm.

Having safe drinking water was a must for my folks—even I understood that—and so we walked toward the truck, dismissing this farm as our future home. Mother seemed relieved to have a good reason not to take this farm. But as we were about to get into the truck, an older man drove up. He got out of his truck rather friskily for his age, shook hands with Daddy and Mother, tweaked my nose, and then through snuff-stained teeth smiled and said, "Howdy! Name's Frank Williams. I live about a mile up yonder," he said, gesturing toward the west.

"Howdy, sir. I'm Tillman Dowden. Good of you to stop by. The large white house on the corner, you say?"

I remembered passing by Mr. Williams's house that morning. The house and all of the farm buildings around it had peeling white paint.

Answering Daddy, Mr. Williams continued, "Yep, that's the one. Right nice house. Built by my daddy in 1901, not long before he up and died of a ruptured appendix. Well, anyhow, mighty glad you folks are looking at this here place. It'll be nice to get some young blood around this part of the county."

"That's good to know, Frank, but we're just about to leave and forget this place on account of there's no drinking water."

On hearing that, Mr. Williams suddenly smacked the palms of his hands together so hard that I jumped and Daddy and Mother looked at him with widened eyes. We remained speechless until his next outburst.

"Well, hold your horses! Uh-h-h, Tillman, didn't you say?" Daddy nodded. Then Mr. Williams informed him that he had heard there once was a well with outstanding drinking water in the pasture half a mile from the house, maybe a little more.

"So let's go have a look," offered Mr. Williams.

"I'm mighty obliged for your interest," answered Daddy as he fell in step with the friendly would-be neighbor. Mother headed to the truck to sit in the cab, where she could bundle up in a quilt against the cold. Unexpectedly, Daddy looked over his shoulder and asked if I wanted to tag along, and so I trotted to catch up with him and Mr. Williams.

I hoofed it as fast as I could next to Daddy, and the three of us set out in earnest to find the well. After a time-consuming search, Daddy became concerned about Mother waiting in the truck all by herself. But just as we were about to return to the house, something almost hidden under a mesquite bush caught Daddy's eye. It turned out it was the well.

Mr. Williams rushed home and brought back a long rope with two wrenches tied on one end for weight, a tin cup, and a crowbar. When Daddy saw all that, he said, "Well, Frank, I see you've done this before."

"Yup," answered Mr. Williams. "Sure have."

After prying off the well's cover with the crowbar, he and Daddy lowered the weighted rope into the well until it touched bottom. When they brought the rope up with several inches of wet on it, they determined the water table was adequate for drinking and cooking. Curious to find out if the water was gyp tainted, they tied the cup to one of the wrenches, lowered the rope again, and brought up some very fine-tasting water. *As good as Arkansas water,* I thought to myself while sampling it.

~

After Mr. Williams left, we walked over to the truck to get out of the wind and talk to Mother. "By dang, there's plenty for drinking and cooking—and we could ask the owner to put in a hand pump," Daddy informed Mother. I could see the glances he cast at Mother, who still seemed far from excited about the prospect of making this particular farm our new home. And I noticed Daddy didn't even mention that we'd have to figure out a way to get the water from the pasture to the house.

He and Mother talked it over, and in the end, although still looking a bit surly, she conceded. "At least the kitchen is bigger than the other two rooms put together," she said. "But I guess we can put our bed in one end of the sitting room, and the baby and Molly May can sleep in the other room. I can make curtains and cover the rough wood walls in all three rooms with something to make them look better, and feel better, too."

"Well, some of the roof shingles on the barn on the north side are missing, but I saw a whole panel of tin stored in the barn. It must have been left over when someone put that tin roof on the chicken coop. I can cut that tin into pieces and patch the holes." Daddy was no doubt hoping this would make Mother feel better about the farm, but she just nodded.

"Now, that barn has a solid loft floor that would shelter cows and horses below, and there's not been any leaking into the south side of the barn. On the west there's a hog pen with a roof on it," Daddy explained excitedly while fixing his gaze toward the barn. I couldn't remember him ever saying so much in only one breath.

He also said that he was sure Ben Fleming could persuade the owner, a rich eastern Oklahoma landowner, who had bought several farms in the area, to agree to pay for a well pump. "But,"

Daddy said, "I doubt Ben Fleming could convince the rich eastern gent to pay for repairs to the barn or the house anytime soon."

I went to bed that night sure we had found our farm. And indeed, the next morning we learned the tenant farmer deal would be finalized on Thursday.

~

"What's a tenant farmer deal?" I asked Mother as we sat waiting for Daddy to sign the papers in the lawyer's office.

"It means your daddy will have to furnish the seeds, the farm equipment, and his hard work. And the landlord will get a hefty amount of the money from the crops," answered Mother with a tinge of disappointment in her voice.

I thought for a while about the landlord's hefty amount of money and wondered how much Daddy's portion would be before I asked, "Will Daddy get enough money to buy anything for us?"

"Oh, yes, I think so," Mother answered. "I think the rains will come, and the dust storms will end pretty soon, and crop prices will be good. And Molly Girl, don't worry. We'll have our milk and butter, and we'll raise our own meat. The landlord won't get any of that." With that, I let go of a good bit of my worry.

~

We quickly moved into the little house in good spirits, with our few belongings and jars of food Mother had earned for helping Mrs. Bridges with her canning. But once we moved in, everyone except the baby admitted that neither the interior nor the exterior of the house had ever felt the touch of a paintbrush.

Fortunately, we were able to put aside our disappointment in the condition of the house and were settled within a day. Since New Year's Day would fall on Monday and school wouldn't start until Tuesday, I had plenty of time to prepare.

The two dresses Mother had fixed up in the summer still fit. Daddy had taken my tattered shoes to the cobbler before Christmas, and they fit, too—tightly. But I had to admit they looked fairly nice. Quite a change from rundown heels, frayed shoestrings, and loosened soles, which had made a flopping sound with my every step—besides causing me to trip and almost fall sometimes.

When I mentioned that the scuffed leather had been polished almost to a shine, Daddy proudly informed me, "The cobbler told me he put extra time on cleaning and polishing your shoes, but he wouldn't charge me, because he was making money hand over fist these days. That's what he said, anyway."

"I'm sure that's because so many people are getting their shoes repaired three or four times before buying new ones. Times are hard," Mother put in while giving me her "you see" look, like she thought I had expected new shoes for school. I hadn't.

Privately I wondered how long the shoe polishing would last. But mostly, I concentrated on trying to be happy about starting school. Deep down inside I was still worried about being the new kid in second grade—and starting in the middle of the school year. I wouldn't know anyone in the entire school, because all of our neighbors were older and their children were all grown up. And to top it all off, Daddy had heard somber news about the school district from Mr. Fleming.

When unwanted or unexpected situations complicated our plans, my folks sometimes said, "That's the fly in the ointment." Mr. Fleming's news about the school certainly fit that saying.

The less than ideal economic conditions had forced the Thistleway School District to cut back on certain expenditures. One of those cutbacks was in the school bus service. What that meant was I would have to walk a mile each way to and from County Road D, where I'd meet my school bus.

Daddy understood the district's position on cutting expenses, but he talked to the president of the school board anyway about the bus picking me up and bringing me home at least when the weather was bad. The man admitted to Daddy that I would have to walk much farther than any other student in the district, but he insisted that the condition of the narrow, rutted road to our house was too poor to send a bus for just one student.

"Poor road!" Daddy fumed when he told us about the meeting. "That's no excuse. The mail carrier drives right by our house six days a week on the same road. And the Elmwood Elementary School District about six miles south of here runs a school bus right by our front door every morning and afternoon."

"That's right," Mother agreed. "Our house is on the north side of the road. If it were on the south side, we would live in the Elmwood District and Molly May would get on and off the bus right in front of our house."

It made no sense in my seven-year-old logic. And with my tendency to worry, it would have been far better if I had never witnessed my parents' concerns about the matter.

My folks also worried because there were no homes closer than a mile from ours in both directions. That meant there would be a long stretch of lonely road between our house and the corner where the school bus would pick me up. But when I recalled the perils Mother had overcome the day she ran with me on her back across the Bradshaw pasture, I decided that, like my mother, I'd keep my eyes peeled and my reaction keen for dangers. And

I figured I'd know how to take care of myself all right without anyone else to help me.

But I had a vivid imagination, and my parents' worry about the lack of transportation spurred that imagination quite a bit. I worried about tumbleweeds rolling down the road on windy days in a group like a herd of stampeding cattle, crashing into me on all sides, leaving their dry, prickly debris on my clothes, face, and neck. I was sure I'd itch the rest of the day. I anticipated days when I would need to squat, close my eyes, and pull my skirt up over my mouth and nose to withstand the assault of a suffocating whirlwind, sometimes rightly called a *dust devil*. I feared my nose and clothes would be full of dust afterward, but I knew from experience that after I coughed several times, I'd be all right.

I also knew there could be other situations that would be beyond my control. What if a stranger would come along in a car and take me away forever? I had heard talk about the Lindbergh child who had been kidnapped, and that made me shudder. Or what if I were caught in a terrible dust storm and Daddy couldn't find me? And what if a neighbor's bull would break loose and I couldn't outrun him?

The one good thing was that I wouldn't need to stand at the corner a mile from my home waiting for the school bus in bad weather. There was a gas station on the corner, and the man who ran it told Daddy I could come inside the station to wait for the bus. Daddy even took me to meet the owner, and I was pleased he looked like my bluegrass-singing Grandpa Dryden. He invited me to pick a candy bar from the large glass candy case, which I had probably eyed much more obviously than I realized. When I hesitated to accept his offer, he said, "Don't worry, I wouldn't let your Daddy pay for it." So I figured I might feel all right waiting for the bus in his station.

~

In spite of the several days I'd had to prepare myself, I was anxious the night before my first day of school. While I helped Mother with the supper dishes, she seized the opportunity to tell me some things about my school building and its history. "Your little white school building was built a long time ago, even before Oklahoma officially became a state."

"When did Oklahoma become a state? Is it really old?" I was curious.

"Oh, ha-ha," she said, laughing. "In 1907. That's close to the year I was born."

I had never thought of Mother as old, but I did wonder if the school building would seem as old as our house.

"Anyway," Mother continued, "a long time ago your schoolhouse was a one-room school for grades one through eight. And imagine this, just one teacher for all eight grades!" She shook her head, as if she herself couldn't believe such a thing. "And here's something else. There were no school buses then, and some children had to walk a good bit farther than you will, my child."

"Will there be only one teacher in my building?" I asked anxiously, still trying to picture myself in that school.

"No, your building is divided into two rooms now—one room for first grade and one for second," she explained. "And third through eighth grades are in the two-story brick building across from the playground."

By the time Daddy came in from milking our two new cows, I felt like Mother had filled me in on all I needed to know. I was more excited than worried now, and I was ready to go to bed for a good night's sleep before my big day.

The next morning when I was all set to walk alone to the school bus, Mother kissed my forehead and said, "Molly Girl, I was smart in my books." Then she swallowed like she had a sore throat before she continued, "Remember, I've always told you you're smart in your books, too."

Of course I liked to learn, but I had a feeling there would be some scary things ahead of me. *Flies in the ointment*, I told myself, but I marched off to school bolstered somewhat by Mother's confidence in me.

~

All the way to the bus corner that morning, I tried to see myself in the classroom surrounded by about twenty kids my age; and since I was starting in the middle of the school year, I was pretty sure I wouldn't be able to do anything as well as the other students in my class. But I told myself I'd try very hard to catch up, and I hoped that no bad surprises were waiting for me on my first day at school.

~

When I entered the classroom, the students were talking in pairs or groups while waiting for the bell to ring. One boy who stood alone looking at the floor seemed about as tall as a sixth-grader, but soon my attention turned to the rest of the students. All of them, except three, were skinny like me.

That was a good surprise.

Two of the three students who were not skinny were girls wearing pretty clothes. They looked like the cute, plump-legged Morton salt girl, but without the umbrella and trail of salt. The third one, a boy, didn't seem quite as plump as the girls. I thought he was the cutest boy I'd ever seen, in his starched shirt, brown suspenders, knickers-style brown trousers, and beige knee-high socks. I hung around close enough to hear another boy call him Frederick.

Before the bell rang, the teacher, Miss Ray, approached me to introduce herself. She took me to a long table with six chairs, patted the back of the chair that would be mine, and said, "This will be your chair. I hope you will enjoy sitting next to Mary Sue." She pointed at the plump, pretty, dark-haired girl dressed so nicely.

By the time the bell rang, I had wandered a little away from my assigned chair to look at a bulletin board, but I quickly returned to my table. Mary Sue and some of the others assigned to my table had not sat down yet, and when I paused for only a moment to consider which chair I'd been assigned, about seven kids told me where to sit. Some of them were wrong about where I was supposed to sit, and I was embarrassed that I couldn't remember which chair was mine. So I just waited until Mary Sue sat down.

I felt lucky to be sitting next to Mary Sue. She smelled like Camay soap. I had smelled Camay soap at Mr. and Mrs. Bridges's home. At our house, we didn't have much water for bathing, and we always used Lava soap. Its texture was rough, as if it had sand in it, and it didn't leave a pretty smell, either. Enjoying Mary Sue's pleasant scent helped me get over my first-day jitters.

I quickly discovered that my classmates were eager to tell me what to do, or what not to do, every time we moved from one activity to another. They even seemed to want to supervise my morning recess activities. All that surprised me, but I decided they might be doing it because they liked me and wanted to be helpful.

At lunchtime my eyes did a double take at the two well-dressed girls' colorful store-bought lunch pails, one red, the other one lilac, both with pretty flowers painted on them.

Mother had washed a small-size empty Karo syrup pail and painted my name boldly on one side of it. The difference between my lunch pail and theirs was a surprise, but not a bad surprise. The bad surprise came when I opened up my lunch.

I discovered my pint-sized Mason jar of milk had tipped sideways and leaked. My biscuit and side pork sandwich and delicious homemade sugar cookie were a mess of mush. Although it was wet with milk, the enticing fragrance of the vanilla in my milk-soaked cookie encouraged my longing to eat it anyway. But I knew I couldn't be seen eating mush with my fingers!

As I fought back my tears and my dread of almost starving by the end of the day, I faked chewing so the others would think I was eating. Luckily though, for the first time since the starting bell had rung that morning, no one seemed to be paying any attention to me. I used my moment of privacy to eye the display of fruit on the table in front of Mary Sue, Jane Ellen, the other fancy-dressed girl, and Frederick. While I anticipated their biting into the fruit, I sneaked looks at them munching their peanut butter on bakery-made white bread sandwiches and sipping their milk. The kids with lunches that looked very much like mine before the milk flood, glanced longingly at the fruit display from time to time, too, and then quickly looked away. I did more than glance. My mouth actually watered. I quickly swiped my mouth with my wrist and, furious with myself, I thought how embarrassing it all was. But I hadn't experienced my worst surprise yet.

~

The final activity of the day was art. The teacher began by saying, "Class, do you remember when we started a new art activity just before Christmas and we used a pattern to trace a big white star on a blue sheet of construction paper? The last day of school before the holiday, remember?"

Everyone chorused, "Yes, Miss Ray." Then she asked Frederick and another student to distribute the students' projects.

Everyone, except me, received a sheet of blue construction paper with a very large white star drawn on it. Their names were printed in the bottom left corner of the blue sheet, and I figured I'd simply missed that assignment and I shouldn't worry. In any case, I was too shy to ask the teacher if I should have materials so I could catch up on the project. My classmates paid no attention to my empty hands, and I guessed they had the same thought: *Molly May missed the boat.*

Miss Ray printed, "Good Behavior Stars," on the blackboard and said, "This says, 'Good Behavior Stars.' Now, everyone print these words in black crayon across the top of your blue sheets."

For want of something to do, I soon peeked to see how Mary Sue was doing. Of course I had no idea I shouldn't look at her paper until she suddenly yelled right in my face, "Copy cat, copy cat!"

I had never heard that expression before, but I knew she meant I'd done something very wrong. My eyes scanned the faces of the other students. All eyes were on me, and I could see their jaws had dropped. Their expressions seemed to say they thought I was the one who'd had the hissy fit, instead of Mary Sue. But *I* was the one dying a thousand deaths right in front of everyone.

That was definitely the worst bad surprise of the day.

But my mind soon was eased a little when the teacher said, "Why, Mary Sue, shame on you. You know Molly May wasn't here the day you all traced your stars." Then to me she said, "Molly May, I'm very sorry I forgot you hadn't even been here that day. I should have given you your materials so you could work on your own star while the rest were doing their printing."

I decided right then I'd never tell my folks everything about my first day at school. I figured I needed to fend for myself. Besides, my acquired wisdom told me my folks already had plenty to worry about.

~

Although I tried to keep my problems to myself at home, a few weeks later something happened at school that I couldn't quite handle on my own. I needed Mother's support. A girl from another class had come to me on the playground and asked, "How come you don't talk like a hillbilly?" Then looking around to see if anyone was near, she leaned closer and asked, "Do hillbillies marry their cousins?"

I hadn't realized that we were considered hillbillies, wasn't certain if it was a bad thing or not, and sure didn't know what the question about marrying cousins was all about. So when Mother and I were doing the supper dishes that night, I told her about the incident. Mother's right eyebrow rose, and she said, "I suppose a cousin marrying a cousin has happened sometimes." Then clearing her throat, she added, "And I suppose in biblical times cousins sometimes married because they usually didn't travel very far to meet other people. So to meet anyone who wasn't a relative sometimes wasn't easy."

I nodded.

"Do you remember the time when we saw two or three young chickens pecking at the head of another young chicken just because its comb was bleeding from an earlier injury?"

I nodded again, still worried.

"Well, if you let what other kids say hurt you, there might be others who will want to peck at your injury, too."

Those words startled me.

"But I'll tell you this," Mother continued, "my family name is Dryden, and your daddy's family name is Dowden, and the *D's* and the *den's* in our names do not make us blood kin. Not in the slightest."

That was good enough for me.

A few days later I had a chance to test my budding sense of family pride and personal identity when a fourth-grade boy named Billy suddenly appeared at my side. While he walked with me the short distance from the school bus to the playground, he smiled and asked, "Do you know what an Oklahoman says to anyone from Arkansas who doesn't shut the door behind him?"

"No-o-o, but you can tell me if you want," I answered.

I was surprised by my good-faith reply, but he did seem genuinely friendly. Still, I braced myself for what he might say.

"They say, 'Shut the door, Arkansawyer.'"

"Why do they say that?" I asked.

He explained that some Oklahomans think hillbillies' houses are built on a hillside and the door just closes by itself.

"I've never seen a house leaning like that on account of it being on a hillside," I said. "And people in Arkansas are too smart to build houses on a place that isn't flat."

Then I looked him in the eye, and I think I grinned. He looked me in the eye, definitely grinned, and said, "My grandparents came here from West Virginia in the early 1900s, and when my daddy was a boy he was asked all the time if his kinfolk in West Virginia made and sold moonshine whiskey."

I almost laughed, and he did, too. "See you!" he said and ran off to join a group of older boys organizing a basketball scrimmage on the court next to the playground. Whether or not I was a hillbilly never worried me again, and I put all of my attention on my schoolwork.

~

By February, dust storm weather reared its ugly head, and that made me fearful I'd be caught in a dust storm while walking to or from the school bus. Maybe I was just getting used to them, but the dust storms in 1934 seemed to be less frequent and less troublesome than we'd experienced the year before. Nevertheless, dust sifted on and into everything.

~

Then, on May 9 that year, a ferocious dust storm struck. It hit while I was at school, not long before afternoon recess. And I'll never forget it.

"We'll stay inside this recess because the wind is blowing the dust outside real hard. The school buses will be picking you up right after recess to take you home before it gets worse," Miss Ray announced.

We put our books into our satchels in preparation for going home. Miss Ray placed crayons and coloring books on each table, and in no time every student's attention was on coloring. Except mine. I needed to pee, and the toilet was outside.

Because the classroom windows were small, high up on the wall, and coated with dirt from other dust storms, I couldn't determine how bad it was outside. Knowing it would be a long time before I'd be home, I decided to brave the dusty winds and make a run for the toilet.

Because it was recess, I figured I didn't need to ask the

teacher's permission to leave the classroom, and I glided toward the exit door. I stopped first by the cloakroom next to the exit to slip on the lightweight sweater I'd worn that morning walking to the school bus. As I stepped toward the double exit doors, I felt good exercising my independence by going outside alone when no one else was out there.

The double doors were thick and heavy. I turned one doorknob while pushing against the door with my other hand, but it didn't open. I tried the other door, and it wouldn't budge, either. Double doors reminded me of church, where the doors were always open for services. And at recess Miss Ray normally opened both of the doors of our little white school building. Surely, I thought, I could open one of the doors somehow. I pushed again and again, taking turns at each door.

Finally, as I was pushing my shoulder as hard as I could against one door, turning its knob at the same time, it suddenly flew open. I stumbled outside and ended up facing the entry. Instantly, the wind slammed the door shut, and somehow three of my fingers got caught in the door. The pain was shocking, and I knew I was in trouble.

I quickly realized that in my haste I hadn't taken the time to button my sweater. The wind was whipping it over my back and flapping it wildly against the back of my neck. I leaned as close as I could to the door, grasping the outside doorknob with my free hand to help steady myself. And, although my trapped fingers hurt, they helped to anchor me so the wind couldn't toss me about like I was an empty paper bag. Still, at times the wind flung me about some, and my trapped fingers hurt even more. Worse, the cold wind was making me need to get to the toilet even more urgently.

I called for Miss Ray as loudly as my bashful nature would

allow, waited, called again, and again, but of course, no one could hear me.

Reality struck me. Neither my teacher nor my classmates had seen me leave, and in the controlled chaos of recess they wouldn't notice my absence. I was stranded outside until recess would end. I cried quietly, and the wind blew my tears against the hand that clutched the doorknob. I pictured Daddy running lickety-split to release my fingers and take me home to Mother.

After what seemed like a very long time, the door suddenly opened and Miss Ray stood with her mouth agape for a moment before she said in a half-crying voice, "Why, Molly May, here you are, here you are. Frederick said he thought he heard you coughing outside the door. But no one saw you leave. Oh-h-h, I'm so sorry."

Before I knew what was happening, Miss Ray had placed one of her arms around the backs of my knees and the other around my shoulders and was carrying me as if I were a baby into the warm safety of the cloakroom. At first I was startled that her plump shoulder felt so different from Mother's thin one, but in the next instant I clung to her, crying quietly and smearing dust-stained tears and snot on the front of her lovely pink blouse.

When she finally set me on my feet and had wiped my dusty, tear-stained face and my runny nose with her pretty, lace-trimmed, pink handkerchief, she said, "Let me take a look at your fingers." I extended my hand. When she had finished manipulating my fingers, she seemed relieved. "Thank goodness, none are broken," she said, smoothing my hair with her fingers while guiding me toward the classroom. But I pulled back and whispered, "I need to use the toilet." And she softly responded, "I'll take you to the storage room commode. We'll need to go through the classroom to get there; just hold my hand."

My silent, puppy-faced classmates' eyes followed us as we hurried toward the storage room. But in spite of their gentle faces, my face burned with embarrassment. Thanks to Miss Ray, I was soon behind the closed storage room door.

When I finally came out of the storage room and returned to the classroom, I could see at a glance that my classmates' faces still looked kind.

But my face burned again when Miss Ray guided me to the front of the room and then said, "Children, I forgot to tell Molly May we have a commode in the storage room for students to use during a dust storm."

For a moment everyone looked at the teacher, surprised by her admission of guilt, but then about three students in unison chirped, "But Miss Ray, we shoulda told Molly May about the commode in the storeroom, too."

"S-h-h! Yes, yes, maybe," Miss Ray answered. "But I think at times some of you are actually just bossing her around, and from now on, I'll be the one to do the bossing, if anyone needs it."

Everyone looked at me again, and I wanted to vanish right through the wood floor.

"Now, Frederick," the teacher continued, "please look in the top left-hand drawer of my desk for the first-aid kit and bring it to me."

Frederick wasted no time finding the first-aid kit while Miss Ray examined my fingers once again.

"Here it is, Miss Ray," said Frederick. "I can help you doctor up Molly May's fingers, if you need any help."

The teacher smiled at him and patted his head. My classmates were still attentive, and Miss Ray seized the moment to inform them that due to the worn-down edges of the very old doors, my slender fingers had been stuck tight between them and had been bruised, but not cut or broken. During her explanation to the class, she glanced at me every little bit and smiled, and strangely, I could barely feel the pain in my fingers. Then she looked at Frederick and said, "Now, Doctor, shall we take care of the patient?"

The good teacher and the cutest boy in the world tenderly wrapped all four of my fingers together as one with gauze and tape. I held my breath as I stole a few bashful glances at Frederick.

~

For the rest of the year, I continued to finish my schoolwork quickly—and accurately. All of my returned assignments and my workbook pages were marked with Miss Ray's red pencil announcing "100%" at the top. I had plenty of time to do most of my homework in class—or do extra-credit reading in books Miss Ray would loan to me. My classmates had completely stopped their bossiness. School life was truly shaping up to my vision of what it was supposed to be, in spite of the dust storms that continued off and on until the end of the school year. I wanted to believe that by summer things would be better for my parents, too.

~

Because school had been dismissed several times that year due to dust storms, classes lasted into the first week of June. On the final day of school, Mr. Williams, who happened to be going to town to buy supplies, drove by my school at noon to drop off Mother and my baby sister, Lettie Ruth.

All of the mothers of second-graders came that noon, each

bringing a dish to pass, plates, and silverware. Miss Ray came prepared to furnish glasses of lemonade. Additional chairs had been brought in from storage and arranged in a semicircle that rimmed one-half of the room. The classroom tables assembled at the other end of the room created a buffet space for the food. The food looked and smelled wonderful, and I could hardly wait to fill my plate.

Soon everyone, including the mothers, sat in the chairs holding their plates heaped with food, and I noticed most of the skinny students' plates were brimming with food, too. And that made me feel better about my almost overflowing plate.

To me, Mother had never looked prettier, with her shining copper hair and her ivory complexion without one freckle. Most of the time, Lettie Ruth was at her best in terms of baby manners. She sat prettily on Mother's lap and never once tried to grab food from Mother's plate or mine. Everyone took turns clamoring for my little sister's direct attention and her quick smile. Once, she dazzled Mary Sue when she blew spit bubbles like I had taught her to do, but I had not intended for her to do it in public. I was a little embarrassed until Mary Sue and those sitting nearby smiled at her.

When Frederick came close to her and said, "Howdy, little Lettie," she responded with, "Ah goo," which was as close as she could come to saying, "I'm good," as I had taught her. I was so happy my baby sister was in the limelight and loved it. I was proud that she wasn't at all shy like me.

But by the time that very special day was over, I knew I wasn't as shy as I had thought. After the mothers had put away their dishes and utensils, and the students were growing tired of their prolonged, reasonably quiet behavior, Miss Ray played the piano and we children sang "My Country 'Tis of Thee" and a couple more songs. I could feel myself singing with gusto, louder than most kids near me.

After our songs, Miss Ray presented some awards to students. I was given a certificate for reading the most take-home books borrowed from the third-grade library, and she announced that I also had read harder books that she had borrowed for me from the fourth-grade teacher. I also received a certificate for being the "most improved student in second grade." Then, as if that hadn't been enough excitement, when the teacher gave the mothers their children's report cards, my mother put her face against mine and whispered, "You got all *A*'s again in every subject, Molly Girl!"

I glanced at my report card and probably smiled, and Mother leaned closer to me and whispered, "Told you you'd always be smart in your books."

~

Daddy came for us in the horse-drawn wagon that afternoon. Since everyone had already left, Miss Ray walked with us to the wagon, where Daddy was waiting. Before we had gone more than a couple of steps, Miss Ray looked at me and said, "Molly May, I'm going to miss your pretty face always paying close attention in class, and I want you to also know that you have no reason whatsoever for being shy."

Because I had heard Mother say "Pretty is as pretty does" a few times, I felt uneasy with Miss Ray's words. Not that I actually ever thought I was pretty. But I knew for sure I was shy, and I promised myself I would work on that, just as I had when I sang with gusto.

When we reached the wagon, Miss Ray quickly extended her

hand to Daddy and said, "I'm Caroline Ray, and I'm glad to meet you, Mr. Dowden. I'm happy to say it's been a joy to have your daughter in my class. She's a very good student."

Her remark certainly reinforced my vow to work on my shyness, and I knew it had jump-started Daddy's sense of humor when he instantly responded, "Thank you very much, Miss Caroline. Yeah, thank you very much. She gets that from me."

My parents and Miss Ray laughed, and I think I might have laughed for a split second, too, and Lettie Ruth smiled as if she understood.

We had traveled homeward for only a few feet when Mother showed Daddy my report card and certificates. He looked at them and then at me with a big grin. After that, he looked toward the northwest sky and said, "Looks like rain clouds over yonder in the northwest, and the cotton I had to replant after the May 9th dust storm is coming along pretty good. A good rain would give it the boost it needs. Yes, sirree, things might be taking a turn for the better!"

It was good for me to witness Daddy's uplifted spirit. I would never forget the damage to the young cotton plants during the May 9th dust storm. The following morning, he came into the kitchen, where Mother and I were making breakfast, slumped into a chair, and moaned, "Blew the cotton plants right out of the ground on the east slope. They're probably landing somewhere in Iowa right about now." Then he stood up and said with an urgent look in his eye, "I have to go see Mr. Fleming about a loan to buy seeds for replanting, in case we get a little rain this summer."

~

"In case we get a little rain" seemed to be constantly on the lips of the local farmers the summer after I finished second grade; some folks said they hoped for downpours. But Daddy said downpours weren't as good as a gentle rain that lasted for a while. I didn't like downpours; sometimes they were preceded by a scary-looking northwest sky that signaled a tornado, which usually occurred around evening milking time. Twice that summer, while my folks were milking the cows, a dark cloud appeared low in the sky. Both times, Mother's voice from the cow lot wafted through the hot air to me in the house: "Moll-e-e-e Ma-a-a-ay! Light the lantern, and get yourself and the baby to the storm cellar-r-r-r! We'll be right there."

Faced with the reality of going to our cellar, I remembered the times when we lived in the shanty and we had to go to Mr. and Mrs. Bridges's storm cellar when it looked like a tornado might hit. Their cellar was made entirely of concrete. Nice. *Our* storm cellar was a dungeon, the home of hideous beasts.

The dungeon was located about eight feet from our back door, and it had two trapdoors on the side facing the house. Beneath the trapdoors were loose wood boards that covered dirt steps leading to a hangout for centipedes, spiders, stinging scorpions, and who knew what else.

Actually, the cellar could have been described as a square hole in the ground covered with boards and a rounded mound of dirt on top. Weeds and prairie grass were allowed to grow thick on the mound to keep it solid in wind and rain—not that there was much rain, and not that weeds needed much rain to grow profusely. But their hardy growth didn't make the cellar seem any less threatening to me.

Lizards with bodies ten or eleven inches long and equally long tails seemed to constantly race out of the growth-covered mound and streak across the closed cellar doors; then they'd circle back through the weeds and grass. I'd seen pictures of racetracks in the newspaper, and I wondered if this was theirs.

"Harmless lizards," I was told, but they made me jump practically out of my skin every time I saw one. They always reminded me of storybook dragons. So with the hyperactive, trespassing "dragons" zipping all around the cellar on the outside and black-and-orange-colored centipedes and other scary permanent residents inside, I never went near it. That is, unless I was ordered to do so when a tornado seemed to be brewing or when Mother asked me to get a jar of canned vegetables from the cellar shelves.

~

We were lucky. Our farm was never struck by a tornado. But the one fairly good rain we had that June caused us to swing into action.

Because baby chicks drown easily in rain, we had to chase down young chickens that had strayed too far from their mothers and the shelter of the chicken coop. The mother hens, sensing the impending danger, had done a fine job leading the chicks that were near them into the coop. But Mother and I had to run helter-skelter to gather the chicks that had strayed too far and deposit them in the nick of time into the mother hens' care. We didn't lose one chick in that June episode, or in any of the few rainfalls throughout the years that followed. Mother often said, "It's partly because you're such a fast runner, Molly Girl."

Even a light rain could cause me to quickly stretch an oilcloth over Lettie Ruth's crib and rush around finding pans and buckets to catch the rain that would rapidly be dripping right through our ceilings. I felt proud when I managed to get a container under every leak in the three rooms. I was especially proud when I had placed containers in the exact spots on our beds where the leaks would have soaked them. Mother praised me for remembering exactly where the leaks were throughout the rooms, in spite of the long period between the rains. "You have the memory of an elephant, Molly Girl," she liked to say. She said it quite often for one reason or another, too, and I liked to hear it.

Leaking ceilings were among the "lemons" we were given with the house, but it could be said that we made lemonade out of that situation. We carefully strained each container of water until it was clear, and then we saved that water to add to our baths or, more likely, for final shampoo rinses. "Rainwater's a good hair conditioner, or it makes a soothing bath," Mother would often say.

After I had taken my weekly bath or washed up at the kitchen washbasin each night, Mother, for reasons I never understood, sometimes took it for granted that I had not done a good job of getting the dust scrubbed off my neck or cleaned out of my ears. And when she took over, she scrubbed and dug so hard it hurt.

Mother was a strong believer in reusing our bath and laundry water to wash the floors in the house and the porch. Sometimes after severe dust storms, Mother used the saved laundry or bath water to wash the dust from the outside of the windows. When the job was finished, we could see the outside world through slightly soap-filmed panes of glass. Mother tried to polish the windows dry with old crumpled newspapers. She claimed the ink in the print made a shine on the windows, and it saved her from having to wash a bunch more cleaning rags.

~

Carrying pails of drinking and cooking water from the well in the pasture to our kitchen wasn't my favorite duty. Operating the pump was difficult for me, and by the time I had pumped two one-gallon buckets full to the rim, I was tired. And before I had walked a dozen steps with the wirelike bucket handles cutting into the palms of my hands, I would forget to be careful, and I would slosh out some of the water.

If I lost too much water by the time I reached the house, Daddy would say, "Go back and pump a couple more buckets and bring them back full." *Pure slavery!* I thought. Yet I knew I had to change something besides my attitude, and I made pads from rags to protect my hands from the thin wire handles.

More to my liking than carrying water was helping Mother all I could with washing clothes on the scrub board, ironing, cleaning, cooking, and taking care of my baby sister.

I had to admit to myself that being active warded off any chance for loneliness and sadness to set in on me. I was relieved that the feelings I'd had after the black widow spider incident hadn't returned. *Now* was different, I assured myself. School and living in our own house, regardless of how crude it was, filled me with purpose. I was happy. Content. Second grade was behind me, and I felt important helping Mother. She usually praised me rather than criticize me for things I could have done better.

My help gave Mother enough time to finish making curtains for all of our three rooms and to help Daddy hoe the cotton. I stayed inside and took care of Lettie Ruth, and Mother came to the house often to cool off and nurse her. But there was one thing that couldn't be done: she didn't have enough time or money to do anything about the ugly walls.

~

The end of July marked the seventh month we had lived on our farm, and one night after he had eaten his supper, Daddy rubbed his brow for a good while and then said, "It's clear the weather's no longer friendly to farmers—or to anyone. Most days the temperature is scorching. As to the rain, a light spring shower and the one quick rain we had only caused the weeds to grow bigger and stronger than the cotton. Bottom line, your mother and I are spending many hours hoeing weeds in the field."

But before long, Mother's talk of having a decent-looking house and Daddy's worry about the weather, hoeing, and crop prices became the least of our concerns. Our darling baby, Lettie Ruth, a normally healthy and happy baby, began to have spells of pain that caused her to draw her knees to her stomach and her hands to flail and quiver. In my parents' opinion, her symptoms went beyond colic. Besides, she was past the colic stage. The doctor had come to check her more than once, and he couldn't determine what was causing her so much pain. He agreed with my parents' observations: it wasn't colic.

"The look of pure shock on her face and her writhing body are not typical of ordinary baby fussiness," said the doctor, and he prescribed a pain medication. *Paregoric*, it was called, and I heard it mentioned often in our house during Lettie Ruth's illness and in later years when Mother felt like talking about it.

For hours, Lettie Ruth's spells would come and go, then stop completely for a few days, and then strike again. I was only eight years old, but I knew that when my beloved baby sister was not sleepy from the medication and was in a pain-free period, she enjoyed anyone who took notice of her, especially her family members. I'd also heard Mrs. Williams and other neighbors comment on her beauty and her winsome personality.

But sadly, at barely nine months old and when she was just beginning to walk, little Lettie's bouts with pain became more frequent and severe, and her brave little fight soon ceased. No more baby smiles and chatter. No more crying in terrible pain. Our little Lettie Ruth lay still and silent. Mother, in spite of her tears, said in a shaky voice, "As her big sister said soon after she was born, 'She brought beauty into our lives,' and that beauty will live on in our hearts forever." And that may have helped us through our first moments of shock and grief.

It happened that the doctor came for the second time that morning, and he arrived within minutes after Lettie Ruth's last breath. We had just finished kissing her good-bye.

"I couldn't get your baby off my mind," said the doctor, sounding out of breath, "and I came back to examine her stomach again." Then the elderly doctor, looking sadly at our Lettie Ruth lying so still, examined the area around her stomach and determined it was bloated. Then on listening to my folks describe her symptoms toward the end—the convulsion and all—he rubbed his brow for what seemed like a very long time.

Finally he said, "She may have been born with *malrotation* of the upper intestine. Which means," he went on, "her intestine was not able to stay where it belonged all the time, and this time it twisted around itself. That was too much for her. Her temperature rose, and she went into a convulsion. Her heart just couldn't take it."

Then he mentioned that some people have lived out their entire lives with that same birth defect and never experienced any severe problems. That left me wondering why our little Lettie had not been one of those fortunate few. I couldn't stop my eyes from automatically turning toward Lettie Ruth, wanting to see her chest rising and falling in fortunate, sweet sleep. Mother's and Daddy's eyes fixed on her, too, as if they felt the same cruelty of fate and wanted deeply to wish it away.

The doctor asked my parents if he should notify the undertaker as soon as he returned to Thistleway. Mother and Daddy could only move their heads up and down slightly to signify a yes.

After the undertaker had come and taken away my baby sister, Mother lay down on the bed. She was exhausted. Although scarcely anyone had a telephone or drove around very much in those days, the news of our tragedy spread quickly. Neighbors came to check on all of us, but to check on Mother in particular. I stationed myself right outside the bedroom door so I could see all that went on when Mrs. Gwen, from north of us, and Mrs. Drecker, who lived up the road to the east, began their tender care. From the open door, I could see them bathing Mother's legs and feet with cool well water because they were swollen from her sitting in the rocking chair with little Lettie in her arms for the many hours she had been critically sick and in pain.

Mother's breasts were painfully engorged with milk, and the ladies covered them with hand towels soaked in cool water, wrung out just enough so there were no drips. Later Mrs. Williams came with a breast pump and helped Mother pump out some of the milk, healthy milk that Lettie Ruth had been too sick to nurse.

Deeply sad because my baby sister was not there to nurse that good milk and frightened about Mother's condition, I reminded myself that it seemed to make Daddy and Mother feel even sadder when I cried. So I thought to myself, *I will not cry. I will not cry.*

Controlling my feelings was difficult. My mind went back to when one of our cute, fluffy baby chickens had died and Mother and I put it in a little box and buried it next to the chicken coop. She assured me the little chicken would be safe and happy that way. Well, I'd heard enough to know my precious little sister would be put in a pretty white casket that would be lowered into a wooden box with a tight cover and then buried in the ground.

That was hard to accept, and it was also hard knowing that the cemetery was seven miles from us and we wouldn't see her smile or hear her jabber sweetly ever again. She'd be lonely, too.

Finally, those thoughts became too much for me, and I hurried out the front door and headed for the back of the house. That way, Mother and Daddy wouldn't hear me cry if I wasn't able to contain my grief. But the sound of sobbing made me stop just before I turned the corner. I peeked around with one eye and saw Daddy standing with his forehead pressed against the side of the house, holding his red bandanna handkerchief over his face, and not because the dust was blowing, either. Then I noticed his shoulders were shaking, and I turned and went back into the house.

I didn't cry. I didn't want my parents to feel worse.

~

When I went back into the house determined to be strong, it was reassuring to see the neighbor ladies still taking care of Mother, just like Grandma Dryden would have done if she were here instead of in faraway Arkansas. I so wished my grandparents were still young and well enough to come see us for a while. I heard Daddy tell Mother that he had paid Mr. Williams the cost of a long-distance phone call to give them the tragic news about Lettie Ruth, but I knew they wouldn't be able to travel the long distance to be here.

I also heard one of the women mention to the others that Mother had told her that the only good dress she had to wear to the funeral was one her husband had bought for her a long time ago in Little Rock. It had large red flowers on a beige background.

Although they were very nice about it, it was plain to see the women thought that dress wouldn't do at all, and Mother seemed relieved to have the decision made for her. Even Daddy, who always said she was the only redhead in the world who looked good in red, quietly told Mother it wasn't right for the funeral.

~

The neighbor ladies and their husbands returned around suppertime with lots of delicious food and plain dark dresses they'd borrowed from their married daughters or daughters-in-law for Mother to try on—and shoes for me to try on, too. Mr. and Mrs. Bridges came later with food and a sack of girls' dresses and shoes from Mrs. Bradshaw.

Shoes! I had been running around barefoot since school had ended, having completely outgrown my old ones.

One of Helen Marie's nice dresses from the sack that Mrs. Bridges had brought fit me. It was a light brown dress with tiny beige stripes. I'd never had a store-bought dress before or a dress with stripes, and I thought I looked very grown-up in it.

I could feel my eyes widen when I saw all the shoes, and I could tell by merely looking at them that Helen Marie Bradshaw's shiny brown shoes were way too wide for my skinny feet. But I hoped, with some feeling of guilt, that all of the other shoes would be much too small for me. Then I could wear Helen Marie's shoes with two pairs of socks to make them tighter.

As "bad" luck would have it, the oldest-looking pair of shoes fit me fine. The ladies looked pleased, and I didn't feel up to suggesting I could wear two pairs of socks in Helen Marie's shoes instead. I reminded myself that the main thing was to be grateful to the ladies for wanting to help us dress especially well for our baby's funeral. To me it seemed like they thought my parents and I were important, and that felt good.

~

The little church was almost full for the funeral. We were not very well acquainted with most of the sad-faced people there, because we were still fairly new to the community. Even the several strangers were so kind to my parents that it seemed like we'd been neighbors all our lives. A number of folks patted me on the shoulder, and I was glad they didn't seem to expect me to talk.

I'm not sure what else, if anything, happened at the church service, except I remember the singing. I was in a daze. Mother and Daddy looked like they were in a daze, too. Yet there was one part of the graveside service I knew I'd remember forever. But for days I wouldn't allow myself to think about it. *Not yet*, I kept saying to myself every time the memory tried to come back to me.

~

Although I remembered the large and beautiful Bridges house and that I had been very self-conscious in the Bradshaws' lovely home, I hadn't actually dwelled on how serious my family's economic situation was. It wasn't until the morning after the funeral, as I listened to my parents' conversation in the kitchen, that I began to acquire some understanding. I heard Daddy tell Mother, "It's a good thing the government check will soon be coming in the mail." Daddy was referring to a check he was owed for plowing under an ill-fated cane field. "The check will pay for the cemetery lot and the funeral expenses, but I reckon there won't be much left after." He took a deep breath before he confessed, "I gave in to Ben Fleming's insisting that he loan me fifty cents from his own pocket so I could buy a new pair of khaki pants to wear to the funeral. I feel guilty about it."

Mother smiled at him and said, "Well, yes, I reckon the days ahead of us will be bad, but better days will come in time. I'm sure of it. Look at this!" She was pointing at their wedding picture, which showed Daddy in a dark suit and tie, and her with very short hair in a loose-fitting black dress with a lighter-colored, shiny trim on the neckline and sleeves. "Flapper style," she said, tapping her finger on herself in the picture. "But with my good cooking," she said, turning to him, "you outgrew this nice suit in a couple of years. Remember, we didn't bring it with us to Oklahoma, and I left the wedding dress in Arkansas for my younger sisters to wear for their weddings."

I knew she was trying to cheer him up, to take his mind off his hurt, but I sensed that he was not yet ready to be cheerful at all. I heard him say he blamed himself for spending too much money on farm equipment, a team of workhorses, and a few cattle and chickens instead of holding back some for harder times. But Mother wouldn't hear of it. "Now, Tillman, no one could have known there would be sickness and death in such a young and healthy family as ours."

Mother's words didn't help much, and Daddy quickly replied, "I should have tried harder to find a used truck with a loan I might have been able to get through Ben Fleming's bank. If I'd had a truck, I could have taken our baby to the University Hospital in Oklahoma City." Ignoring Mother shaking her head, he insisted, "You remember, like one of the well-off farmers north of here did, who had a car. You know, when his boy was real sick?"

"Yes, I heard from Mrs. Williams that the doctors operated on the boy. And that took care of it," Mother answered.

I was worried once again. Up until that time I had no idea that perhaps our financial situation was somehow responsible for my baby sister's death.

A few days later, my folks tried hard to carry on, and they resumed their work in earnest. Still, a persistent pall of sadness hung over our home. It was a heavy load for me to carry. I felt so sad, and after a few more days of pushing back, I finally allowed the details of what happened that day at the graveside to return to me.

~

The minister, Mother, Daddy, and I were standing in front of Lettie Ruth's casket next to the oblong opening in the ground when I looked up and saw a fast-moving whirlwind coming right for us. My folks' eyes were downcast, and they didn't see it coming. When the whirlwind struck, the sound of the dirt hitting the side of the casket and its closed lid caused their heads to pop up. Their eyes widened in alarm when they saw the ghastly trick the whirlwind played. The reddish-tan dust-devil dirt coated the prettily embossed white lid of the casket, cascaded from its rounded edges, and then rolled down the sides. The pure, clean white of the casket, which so represented our darling little baby, was ruined. If this hadn't happened, the casket would have stayed a perfect white inside the wooden box forever—in my mind at least.

My parents' faces during that moment at the grave site came back to me several times in the days that followed. But my recollection of those startling few seconds gradually became dimmer, like an image in a framed picture in a room where the lamp has been turned down low to save on kerosene.

~

The stack of summer books my teacher had loaned to me beckoned me to resume my reading, and I did. From my reading spots in the three rooms, I couldn't help being aware sometimes of my parents' conversations, even when I wanted only to be following the plot of my story. For instance, when Daddy said, "We need a cream separator and an icebox so we can increase the amount of cream and eggs we sell," I lost my place on the page thinking, *Where will the money come from to buy an icebox? A cream separator, too!*

"I know we need to sell more cream and eggs," Mother agreed. "And thank goodness, we bought all that cracked corn for the chickens and feed for the cows before we ran out of money. Milk and eggs are such important foods for us—especially for Molly May. She needs milk three times a day to keep her teeth and bones strong. Even so, we're already putting aside more milk and eggs each day than we can use, and we're getting some income by selling more of them, too."

So far I hadn't been told to help Daddy with the milking, but right away, I envisioned my reading time being cut short because I would be gathering eggs and washing them after school every day. Then I imagined the sound of a monstrous cream separator motor whirling every night and every morning. I wasn't looking forward to that either. I was pretty sure I would be the one turning the crank to make that motor whirl. But those were thoughts I didn't want to dwell on, and I tried not to let them in very often.

As to having an icebox, my attitude was more positive. From hearing my folks talk, I figured neither the cistern nor the storm cellar was cool enough for storing anything for very long, nor was there enough room for extra storage—especially in the cistern. There could be only so many buckets of stuff stored in the cistern right above the water, where it was the coolest. We, or most of the time I, needed to be able to draw up a bucket of water without bumping into any other storage buckets, which would cause them to sway all over the place. The bumping could loosen the lids, so all sorts of dairy products would slosh out into the water, which would make the water turn bad. I had drawn water from the cistern many times and could predict those situations. Daddy could, too. He was the one who had caused the water to turn bad one time.

And indeed, once such a disastrous slopping accident *almost* happened to me, too. That near-disaster taught me a lesson, and after that I'd pull up all of the storage buckets prior to lowering my water bucket. When I had my bucket of water safely drawn up, I then lowered the buckets of dairy products and eggs back into the cistern. More work, less worry. "Toe the mark" was my motto.

~

On nights when Daddy rested for a short while in the sitting room, I'd quietly listen to Mother talk about things that were on her mind while she hand-skimmed the cream from day-old milk. When her skimming task was finished, either she or I would hang the bucket of cream back in the cistern alongside our larger bucket of milk and smaller buckets holding our other perishables, such as eggs. Our cream soured in a few days, but Mother said sour cream was part of our economic plan. Eggs were part of our economic plan, too.

"A few of the town ladies like to make cake and cookies with sour cream and eggs," Mother explained, "and your daddy made an agreement with Mr. Offner at the Thistleway General Store to buy our sour cream and extra eggs, or trade them for groceries." I was glad to have the groceries, but I couldn't help wishing we could have cake made from sour cream and eggs, too.

~

Not long after my baby sister's funeral, I enjoyed my first trip into town alone with Daddy. It turned out to be a good opportunity for me to see a side of him I had never seen before.

The Thistleway General Store had a parrot named Charlie. That bird was about as scruffy-looking as the rain-starved crops, and his voice sounded like he had been in a dust storm or two. Every customer clearly had to take notice of Charlie, or that customer was greeted over and over with the bird's squawky, "Howdy there, Mister." That day he targeted my daddy, but Daddy was too busy bartering with the store owner to respond to him.

Finally, in exchange for Daddy's dozen eggs and pint of thick sour cream, Mr. Offner agreed to let him have a large sack of rice and an almost equally large-size package of dried pinto beans. But he said that Daddy had to give him five cents to boot. Daddy agreed to the deal, but the look in his eyes reminded me of what he had said on the way to town that morning: "Mr. Offner is a bit of a money-grubber."

After the trade was completed, Daddy dug in his pocket for his last penny to buy a handful of peanuts-in-the-shell for me. Only then did he appear to be aware of the parrot. I hoped he was going to get around to doing something to please its owner. I remembered Daddy had told me during our wagon ride to town that he would need to put himself in good standing with Mr. Offner. For on his next trade he would try to get fifty cents cash out of him for a cleaned and cut-up fryer-size chicken from our small flock. Selling the chicken would be a significant sacrifice for us, because we loved our fried chicken and usually had it only on a Sunday.

"I need the money to pay back banker Ben Fleming. He loaned me fifty cents from his own pocket for something I needed in a hurry," Daddy had confided during our trip to town. I knew he was talking about the khaki pants he had bought for the funeral. That morning in the wagon was the first time he had ever said anything to me related to Lettie Ruth's funeral, even indirectly.

All the while Daddy bargained with Mr. Offner that day, my eyes and ears were alert for what Daddy could do to get on the good side of Mr. Offner. Sure enough, after he paid for my peanuts, he stuffed the sacks of rice and beans under one arm, turned to the parrot, and said, "Howdy there, Charlie Boy. How you doing, dude?" Then over his shoulder he said, "Smart bird you've got there, Mr. Offner."

Daddy let Charlie jabber at him for a while; then he tipped his sweat-stained hat. As he pivoted toward the door, Daddy motioned for me to follow.

As soon as we stepped outside, I saw a boy leaning against the building eating an ice cream cone. He was taking long, circling licks and slapping his tongue back into his mouth before the half dozen flies that were circling the cone could land on his tongue. I stopped in my tracks, both awed and repulsed. But quickly Daddy turned around and said, "He's Mr. Offner's grandson. Don't stare." And with that, Daddy peered into the store's display window at the dusty-looking ladies' and girls' dresses. He studied them a few seconds and then looked down at me and said, "Someday when I have enough money, I'm going to buy you and your mother new dresses—hers with red stripes and yours with blue flowers."

I appreciated his words and his generous feelings, but I also figured he wanted to make up for that morning when he had come into the house raving mad, cussing and taking his spite out on Mother. He knew she very much disapproved of swearing, no matter what the reason might be. That morning a cow had kicked over a large bucketful of milk. Such a big waste really got to Daddy. Mother and I understood that. And although I didn't like seeing him angry, I knew it was hard for him to have patience, especially since we left Arkansas and moved to Oklahoma.

He had come to the plains with hope for improvement in our future; yet over a year had passed since our arrival with no improvement in sight. Hope was hard to hang on to. And as hope faded, so did patience. With all the ups and downs of hope, patience, and disappointment, I sometimes felt like a yo-yo.

As Daddy and I were walking from the Thistleway General Store toward our wagon that morning, Mother's words while she was helping me pretty myself for the trip to town popped into my head: "Your daddy always feels better after he's talked to Ben Fleming. I think he feels a little like Mr. Fleming is the father he lost when he was such a young boy. I think maybe Mr. Fleming has a fatherly feeling toward your daddy, too."

Then coincidentally, I saw Mr. Fleming. I had never formally met him, but I remembered seeing him at the funeral. Now he was coming out of the post office headed toward Daddy with his hand extended for a handshake and, I hoped, down-to-earth words of friendship.

"Howdy, Tillman," Mr. Fleming greeted him. "Haven't seen

you for a while. How are the crops doing in this worse-than-ever drought?"

"Well, never enough rain here on the plains," Daddy more or less sang, followed by a grin more natural than I had expected, yet I thought he looked slightly surprised those words had come from him.

"You're a born poet, Farmer Dowden. You sound like that singer … what's-his-name," Mr. Fleming said, laughing. "You should make a whole song of that ditty and sing it on that new radio show, *The Grand Old Opry.*"

Daddy grinned again, and in a serious tone Mr. Fleming changed the subject to President Franklin Roosevelt's New Deal. He assured Daddy that things might soon get better for everyone. Daddy looked at him with a slight scowl, and I wondered why he hadn't looked pleased instead.

"Well, that word, *everyone,* bothers me some," Daddy responded after a pause, "and I figure no matter how long it takes for things to get better again, the farmers who inherited their money and big farms with better soil will already have more money than anyone could shake a stick at when the *big give-away* is split up amongst *all* farmers. And that's how it'll be—just you wait and see."

Mr. Fleming tipped his hat and smiled at a man passing by in dirty overalls, but he quickly looked back at Daddy and said, "That's true, and right now those more fortunate farmers can afford to start over when rabbits, grasshoppers, or a dust storm wipe out their cotton plants."

I knew that Daddy admired men who started out with nothing and worked hard for what little they had, and I held my breath waiting for what he would say next. Sometimes I wished I didn't think all the time; thinking made me worry.

"I know it," Daddy finally replied to the banker's last comment, "but I don't begrudge them none about anything. No, sirree, not as long as they and their young'uns don't act all uppity. Some of them were in Thistleway School with my daughter last term, and she didn't complain about anyone acting uppity."

Daddy's final comment brought me back to how I felt when I first saw Helen Marie Bradshaw dressed so nicely the day Lettie Ruth was born. And I recalled how much I admired Mary Sue's and Jane Ellen's pretty clothes every day in second grade. But I didn't begrudge them, either. I simply wished I, too, could have had nice things to wear and good things to eat, like bakery-bread sandwiches, apples, oranges, and bananas, which would not only taste good but also make me a little more plump and cute.

"But we manage to scrape for food and other necessities," said Daddy, after looking at the ground for a while.

"Aw, I know you do," the kind banker replied sympathetically. "You *are* a good provider, and I'd like nothing better than to see all small-scale farmers buying extras like radios, iceboxes, and automobiles." I visualized a radio and icebox in our house, and the idea alone made my heart leap a bit.

"But the hardworking, small-scale farmers' time will come. So what I'm saying is, Tillman, the Lord knows you're a hard worker. Patience and hope will carry you through."

As the two shook hands, Daddy leaned toward Mr. Fleming's ear and said something so low-voiced I couldn't hear, due to a horse-drawn wagon clanking by us. Mr. Fleming patted Daddy on the shoulder, and I heard him say, "I'm not worried about it. I know you'll pay me back as soon as you can."

I was pretty sure then that they were talking about the fifty cents Daddy had borrowed to buy the new khakis, and I was grateful Mr. Fleming didn't seem to mind the outstanding debt. I knew Daddy felt bad about it—he was such a proud man and did not like being indebted to anyone—but I was glad he had done it so he'd be dressed nice for Lettie Ruth's funeral. My baby sister deserved that. I was sure of it.

~

On the wagon ride home, my mind left the subject of hard times when I noticed that, in spite of the hardships so plain to see that day, Daddy's spirit seemed lighter than usual as he clicked his tongue and snapped the reins to make the horses trot a little faster. All the way home I felt like smiling.

The next day, Mother, Daddy, and I had something to smile about together when a letter came from my school. It was from Principal Armstrong, Miss Ray, and the fourth-grade teacher, Miss Woods. The letter stated that my scores on the end-of-the-year tests had been remarkable, and it suggested that I skip third grade and go right to fourth grade when school resumed in the fall. I thought it would be nice if I were making room for someone who could use more teacher help—and that might be possible for some students, if I moved ahead to fourth grade.

At first, I was surprised by the news, but then I told myself that the girls with cute, plump legs wearing pretty store-bought dresses could neither outrun me nor outdo me in *everything*. So I thought maybe I'd like to skip third grade. Still, I thought if I should skip third grade, I'd not be starting school with classmates I was used to. I'd miss seeing Frederick, too. Not that I ever talked to him or let him catch me looking at him. Well, except for one time.

I had been saving a nickel in a small, empty jar since last April when our neighbor Mr. Williams had given it to me for sweeping the thick remains of a dust storm from the bed of his truck while he talked to my daddy. At the gas station I finally bought a Snickers candy bar with the nickel, and I truly looked forward to taking it from my lunch bucket at noon and savoring its richness. But after I'd eaten my biscuit sandwich, something crazy came over me. I took the Snickers bar across the room to Frederick and thrust it into his hand, saying, "Here, you can have this. I'm not hungry." Frederick looked confused as I twirled an about-face and almost ran back to my seat.

"Thank you," I heard him say softly to my back as I scurried to my chair, feeling my heart beat against my ribs—embarrassed to my core, and really craving that candy bar!

~

With a couple of days to think about the jump to fourth grade, the lure of being with older classmates and doing harder lessons won out, and I shared my feelings about it with my folks. Mother was pleased and said, "You'll do just fine."

Daddy wasn't sure how he felt, but Mother reminded him that I could graduate from high school a year sooner. Daddy seemed only somewhat impressed, and Mother took a different tack and said, "It would save money in the long run. And just think, she'd be able to move to Oklahoma City and get a good job a year sooner."

I could see Mother had energized his attention, and his brow was knit in thought, but I couldn't tell if he approved or strongly disapproved. I waited for Mother to continue. And she did.

"She might meet an educated man with a good job." She glowed while Daddy blinked his eyes and scrunched his forehead. Then she finally said, "And get married, have a brick house, or at least a painted house, with flowers beside the front door and a grassy lawn bordered by big trees. Just think, Tillman, running water in the kitchen. And, my goodness, an indoor toilet!"

Mother should have been a preacher. Daddy was on board, and it all made up for the discomfort I had felt when she talked about my getting married.

~

It was a long walk down our poorly maintained dirt road, but Mrs. Williams would sometimes walk by our house early in the morning—for exercise, she claimed. But if Mother and I happened to be outside hanging clothes on the lines or watering the chickens, she always stopped to visit with Mother for a few minutes.

Because the neighbors had been so good to our family during our tragic loss, Mother was always happy to have a little visit with any of them. "Even if they're older than I am, and they don't have young children you can play with," she confided.

I liked to stand close to Mother and listen to their grown-up talk. But every time there was a visit with Mrs. Williams, one thing always irritated me. Mrs. Williams would lean toward Mother to say, "Your Molly May sure does stand up mighty tall and straight."

Mother always claimed my hearing was as keen as a hoot owl's, and I believed she was right. I certainly caught Mrs. Willams's comment every time, and I would hang back a step behind Mother, feeling self-conscious, thinking, *Boys are supposed to be tall, not girls.* But one time when Mrs. Williams whispered her usual comment, I thought about how Charlie, the parrot at the general store, would repeat the same words over and over to every customer, male or female. I stifled a snicker imagining, "Howdy there, Mister," coming from the parrot if Mrs. Williams happened to be the only customer in the store. I wondered how she'd feel if she were called "Mister." But my moment of glee lasted less than a second before I was ashamed of my hateful thought.

~

One day when Mrs. Williams was back on the road far away enough to be out of hearing range, I didn't curb myself from expressing my thoughts about her usual comment. I turned to Mother and said sassily, "Is it bad to be tall and straight?"

"Aw, she means it in a nice way!" Mother answered, keeping her voice low. But something in Mother's tone told me I had been too big for my britches, and then I heard my inner voice tell me I'd better watch my attitude.

"Well, I know she shouldn't whisper it like it's something not nice about you, something you shouldn't hear," Mother said less critically. "It's just her way. So pay no attention to such words if they make you feel funny. Just be my pretty, tall girl, you hear?"

Now, that compliment on my stature really surprised and pleased me, but she spoiled it when she tacked on, "And keep eating plenty of rice and red beans. Good for your complexion."

~

Rice and beans, rice and beans! It was rice for breakfast morning after morning. Never a bowl of Wheaties, like we'd had one morning when we stayed with Mr. and Mrs. Bridges. It didn't help either that some kids on the playground at school sang their adaptation of the radio commercial jingle that went, "Have you tried Wheaties—the best breakfast food in the land." I imagined a radio jingle about beans, and that made me laugh out loud.

Day after day it made me feel sick to my stomach to smell the dried brown-and-beige-speckled pinto beans cooking in the early stage. But after the beans had cooked for about two or three hours in water with a spoonful of lard—or meat-flavored fat drippings, when drippings were on hand—the beans began to smell like real food. At that point, I would lift the cover to see the beans cooked to a soft doneness, now turned a solid reddish-brown color swimming in thick juice; and Mother's words would seem to float up from the steaming pot: "A daily serving of rice and beans equals a serving of meat."

At mealtime I would alternate from a nibble of corn bread, to a mouthful of red beans, to a bite of onion, to a gulp of milk that calmed the onion's burn. Nonetheless, the onion woke up my taste buds to the flavor and creaminess of the beans, rich in protein. At least Mother said they were full of protein. She also knew the importance of a glass of milk at every meal, and she saw to it that I had mine.

But how easy it was to allow negative feelings to creep in when variety wasn't there! How good it would have been had I known then that dietary guidelines would someday suggest a very small portion of your plate for meat—unless it's fish or fowl—and the rest of your plate for vegetables, fruit, and grain.

Regrettably, I hadn't known at the time that much more than half of my diet was filled with healthy food, albeit not the ideal variety of fruits and vegetables. Raw onion in those days was considered more a condiment than a vegetable, plus it caused bad breath. But I didn't need to worry about that. I didn't have playmates coming to play with me. I would have been glad to give up my raw onion for a day if I could have had a friend come to play.

Little did I know that being void of a playmate would soon change—but not for the better.

~

I had thought a lot about starting fourth grade and making some new friends. Then one morning when Mrs. Williams was walking by our house, she came to the sitting room window and peered through it. When she spotted Mother sitting at her quilting, she called through the screen, "Hello in there, Elsa Ruth. Want me to come in and help you for a half hour or so?"

Mother was so startled she pricked her finger with her needle and yipped, "Ouch," but she instantly recovered. "Why, of course, come on in."

"Are your eyes feeling good enough to be quilting, Elsa Ruth? You had so much trouble with them during the dust storms, I recall," Mrs. Williams asked as she hustled through the door.

Mother told her she had been fine since the dust storms had temporarily subsided.

Then I saw that Mrs. Williams had brought her granddaughter, Vera Lou, with her. I had heard Mrs. Williams say to Mother one time, "Vera Lou's teachers say she isn't dumb. Actually she is quite smart—cunning, in fact. But she never pays attention in school, and she talks funny because she has some kind of speech problem. Well, you know her mother is from the Deep South and her accent is strong, and so is Vera Lou's."

I had seen the girl briefly one time before. She was hitting Mr. and Mrs. Williams's nice old collie dog, Hattie, while visiting their farm. When the poor dog tried to get out of the girl's way, she yanked its long, soft fur and yelled at it. I was afraid to play with her. She attended Elmwood Elementary, was two years older than I, and definitely was a lot meaner.

But alas, there she stood in my house, and I was hard-pressed for toys or dolls for us to play with. She nixed my suggestion to play hopscotch on the hard dirt of our bare front yard. "Ain't what I'm used tuh," she responded sullenly.

I felt a big question mark swirl from the top to the bottom of my face, and I suspected she saw it.

"Well, I play hopscotch at school. It's drawed with chalk on a sidewalk," she announced haughtily.

I didn't tell her I also was used to playing hopscotch at school, and I didn't tell her that I couldn't imagine a southwest Oklahoma farm girl who hadn't played it on her own bare yard. My suspicion about her nature was firming up; I suspected she would slam the door on any suggestion I might make, simply because she was mean. Yet I felt nervous at the thought of our having to sit for a half hour just looking at each other, or worse, trying to ignore each other.

Since Mother at times had invited me to do some quilting, I asked, "Mother, could Vera Lou and I stand at one end of the quilt and do some stitching, too?"

"Why, certainly," Mother answered me, and to Mrs. Williams she said, "Don't worry. My quilting design is simply straight lines. It's nothing fancy like some."

Mrs. Williams looked pleased, and she coaxed her granddaughter to try her hand at quilting. Vera Lou agreed reluctantly, and her grandmother showed her how to stitch along the faintly drawn dotted lines.

The ten-year-old seemed distracted and fidgety while she observed her grandmother's demonstration before she would be allowed to start on her own. But soon she was stitching next to me. I had to admit to myself that she did it quite well, and I finally told her so. She looked at me from the corner of her eye and lip-fluttered "Ph-t-t-t." Then she said loudly, "I'm gonna quit."

She and I moved to the kitchen, where I listened to her drop names of friends like they were as sensational and well known as the child movie star Shirley Temple. I knew about Shirley Temple because Mary Sue and Jane Ellen had shown me pictures of her.

Vera Lou was also very boastful about her school's all-brick building. I didn't feel like telling her I'd be in a brick school building, too. I happened to know her building was only one story high, while mine was two. I wouldn't have told her that either. But since she seemed to appreciate her school and its students so much, I had at least picked up a clue. So I asked, "Would you like to go outside to the shade of the house and play school?"

"There'd be jest one stu-ent," she snarled, making me feel like she'd slammed the door in my face again.

"Could we imagine there are more students?" I asked, too imploringly for a fourth grader, I thought.

Her prolonged silence made me very uncomfortable.

"Yeah? How?" came at last from her tight-lipped mouth.

"Okay, could we take turns pretending to be a smart student— or a dumb one? Or-r-r, maybe a mean one," I added, regretting she was a natural for a mean-student role.

There was another silence until a hen cackled sharply from the chicken coop.

"Well, would you like to be the teacher?" I bargained again with little heart in it, fairly sure she wouldn't be nice like Miss Ray was in second grade, or like I would be if I were the teacher.

Vera Lou's "Nope, don't wanna be no teacher" ended our verbal zigzagging.

I was disappointed she had balked at all of my suggestions. I really wanted us to do something together that would make her feel friendly toward me, even if she might be bossing me around. Finally I remembered that we had a new litter of baby pigs, and I asked Vera Lou if she'd like to see them.

"Yeahhh! But jest in case yuh'd like to know, I hate school and I hate teachers." Then she set off for the pigpen, and over her shoulder she shouted, "Last one there's a piker."

I hadn't heard the word *piker* before, but I figured it meant something like *scared*. Not that I cared very much what it actually meant. I was almost sure I could outrun her, but instead I just trotted along behind her. After all, it wasn't like we were racing to get an ice cream cone.

I would have run as fast as a jackrabbit for an ice cream cone. But I wouldn't run to see baby pigs in a smelly pen, although I thought baby pigs were especially cute, and I liked looking at them—from a distance.

Vera Lou waited for me at the pen, but as soon as I stood next to her, she bolted right over the fence and snatched one of the baby pigs away from its mother. Quick as a wink the mother pig almost attacked her. I held my breath until the wild-eyed girl had done a leapfrog over the fence, while calling the mother pig bad names. I couldn't help thinking I wouldn't have blamed the mother pig if she had nipped Vera Lou's heels before she could get out of the pen. But I was happy that Vera Lou was safe.

We watched the pigs through the fence, as I had intended from the start. But before long Vera Lou turned around and gawked with a half-sneering smile at our barn roof. I could tell her line of vision went straight to the one hole where a tin patch had recently blown off during a wind storm. Daddy had found the piece of tin in the pasture, but he hadn't had time yet to nail it back on the hole.

I had been embarrassed about our barn roof since second grade when I overheard a boy say, "She lives in that place down the road from that filling station out on County Road D. Her place is the one with tin patches on the barn roof."

I imagined a student, someone like Vera Lou, identifying me as the girl whose barn roof had tin patches and one big hole in it, too. But I rapidly put my attention on not allowing shame to show on my face, and I braced myself for hearing another snide comment come from her mouth.

True to form, after she had smirked at the roof for what seemed like ten minutes, she suddenly smiled weirdly at me and asked, "Yer daddy plum run outen tin?"

My faced burned, but she pretended not to notice. Instead, she gave me another crooked smile and said, "Let's go up to duh loft and crawl outen that there hole. We kin set on duh roof and look around."

I shook my head and let a frown crease my brow, but she pretended not to notice and went on, "That there hole's so low on duh roof we kin stand on duh loft floor and climb outen it."

I had thought about doing that very thing the day the wind had blown the tin patch off the roof. But I had quickly thought better of it *then*, and I did not want to do it for Vera Lou *now*. So as nicely as I could, I answered, "You can, but I don't care to."

She rolled her eyes and then gave me a look like she thought I was an awfully timid little soul. I was afraid of her, and I wanted desperately to prove to her I wasn't timid. But instead, I did an about-face and took a step toward my house.

"If yuh don't, yusa piker," she challenged.

She had tossed the word *piker* at me one time too many. I turned around and looked at her, wondering how I was going to get out of sitting on the barn roof admiring the aerial view of the land and at the same time prove I wasn't overly scared. But for a second or two my mind wavered back and forth between giving me the go-ahead and telling me that this was an insane idea. Finally it signaled me to go ahead and enjoy the adventure.

We climbed the rickety steps to the loft and took turns sticking our heads through the hole in the roof. I had to admit to myself that it was exhilarating from up there, until Vera Lou said, "I'd dare da crawl outen there and jump offen duh low edge of duh roof. Lookie, it's not far from duh ground."

She was right—the north and south sides of our barn roof sloped low. I recalled that one day I had enjoyed jumping off a big, upside-down barrel a few times. But I soon quit doing it, because Mother saw me and said I'd break my arches. So to consider a jump off the barn roof caused every bone in my body, and especially my feet, to shout that I shouldn't. I thought for a minute about how to tell Vera Lou clearly, without raising her dander, that I wouldn't jump. Finally I said, "I'd jump off that roof only if it would save my life."

"Well, okie-dokie then, we'll jest set ourselves outen there on that there roof. Right close to duh edge like stupid birds who kin fly but not jump," she agreed cynically. Then, suddenly changing her tone to surprisingly polite, she added, "Yuh kin go first if yuh wanna."

I accepted her pretend gesture of courtesy and climbed out onto the roof. Then slowly, on hands and knees, I crept like a giant tarantula to the edge, sat down, and pulled my skirt up over my knees. Then just as I was feeling somewhat comfortable, I heard a strange sound and looked over my shoulder and saw Vera Lou.

She was still standing on the loft floor with only her head and torso visible above the hole in the roof! Has she changed her mind, I wondered, I hoped.

Then I realized the strange sound I'd heard had been moaning. It was getting louder, and it was coming from Vera Lou. And while my brain tried to tell me what was going on, her head suddenly flopped to one side and her eyes crossed and seemed to bulge like a frog's. Her mouth dropped open, and her tongue hung out of one corner. Then, most scary of all, her arms flailed jerkily. At first I was so dumbfounded I couldn't speak, but I finally squeaked, "What's wrong?" fearful she was suffering from a convulsion like my baby sister had when she was dying.

Before I could get on my hands and knees to crawl to her, she was moaning louder than ever and began to climb in jerky movements onto the roof.

My instinct kicked in. I was almost certain the girl would not have been able to climb if she were in a convulsion. Then I became terrified that she was in some sort of violent fit, and I scooted on my butt to the very edge of the roof and jumped off.

A bit jarred from head to toe from the impact of my miraculous landing on both feet, I was, nevertheless, off and running. But before I had run halfway to the house, I heard Vera Lou laughing. I turned to see her coming out of the barn door, staggering toward me, holding her sides and gasping, "Didja jump tuh save yer life, yuh tall, skinny Arkansas hillbilly?"

"I am not a hillbilly," I practically yelled just because it was Vera Lou who said it, and then I turned toward my house again. But I stopped, turned toward her, and lividly rebuffed, "Chew on this, Vera Lou Williams. I *am* a hillbilly, if you mean my parents and I speak a lot better English than you do." It was a low blow, and I instantly regretted it. Then I spun around toward my house fearing what she would say or do next.

"Yuh hada wear my shoes tuh yer baby sister's fumeral," she shot back.

Her words stung. But images of how Daddy had dealt with the obnoxious mountain boys when he was a youngster flitted across my brain, and over my shoulder but plenty loud enough for her to hear, I huffed, "Too bad we're girls, for you need to get punched in the nose." Then I stopped and faced her, and I think I even shouted, "And if you ever fool with me again, I'm going to pretend I'm not a girl and you're going to get it." And I even took a couple of menacing steps toward her. She looked at me with fear in her eyes and took a few steps backward before she spun around and made a run for the barn. I watched her hightailing it for a second or two before I turned, hiked my chin a little higher, and strolled toward my house. I felt good.

When I reached the door, I stopped and looked back just in time to catch Vera Lou peeking around the corner of the barn and then ducking back like she'd seen the boogeyman.

I waited for a while, watching her face periodically peek and duck. At the same time I felt my shoulders resuming their normally straight posture and my fourth-grader status seeping into every inch of my tall, slender self. I allowed a minute more of my enjoyment to pass before I opened the door and strode briskly into my house, where I found Mother and Mrs. Williams talking about making flour sack dresses. Obviously, they had been too engrossed in their talking to notice the ruckus outside. After they acknowledged me with their glances and faint smiles, I pulled a chair next to Mother and sat down, and Mrs. Williams asked, "Why, where's Vera Lou?"

I shrugged and nonchalantly pointed toward the door. She seemed satisfied and went right back to her talking. Vera Lou finally slouched in, whining, "Grammar, let's go."

~

Cotton material was very inexpensive, and flour mills began selling their flour in floral print cotton sacks. From those sacks, mothers and grandmothers were making school dresses for their daughters and granddaughters with matching underpants called *bloomers*. There were several prints from which to choose. The problem was most families used cornmeal with only a little bit of flour to make corn bread for lunch and supper. Flour was used mainly for breakfast biscuits. So it took a long time for smaller families to use enough flour to save the approximately three to four sacks needed for a grade-school girl's dress and bloomers. Four sacks sounded like a lot, but after the women preshrunk the sacks, there was considerably less material left for the pieces needed to make both the dress and the very roomy bloomers.

Another complication sometimes occurred when the store ran out of sacks of flour in a particular print pattern. But the resourceful community women put their heads together, and each mother or grandmother would go ahead and buy her sack of flour in a different print. Then the women would simply trade flour sacks in order to get enough of their material. So the saving process went faster than it might have otherwise. I felt good knowing my community wanted to cooperate in that way.

The women also saved money by sharing dress patterns. Each woman would vary the style a little. They might change the collar from rounded and small to larger or no collar at all with a narrow bow sewn at the center of the plain neckline. Others changed the sleeve bottoms from cuffs to narrow crochet trim, or simply some elastic inside narrow hems. I could hardly wait for Mother to finish making my new flour sack dress. It would be fun to see if any girls would be wearing dresses of the same print as mine, but even more fun to see those that were different.

~

Because it had been so extremely hot that summer, it seemed like Mother was constantly telling me to remain indoors or, if outside, to stay in the shade. That restriction had made summer vacation drag by, and I looked forward to being in school again. My spirits lifted when Mother finally finished sewing my new flour sack dress and bloomers. I started picturing myself in school among the other girls, and I hoped I hadn't lost the confidence I had gained in second grade—and in the head game I had won with Vera Lou.

I reminded myself that I probably could run faster than just about any other girl. Besides that, Miss Woods, my soon-to-be fourth-grade teacher, and Principal Armstrong had written my folks another letter thanking them for their decision to allow me to be promoted. The letter ended with a special message to me that said, "Molly May Dowden, welcome to fourth grade, school year 1934–1935."

~

One day not long after Vera Lou had made her memorable visit, Daddy returned from town with groceries and some rope to make a jump rope for me. He had the kind of look on his face that signaled there would be a conversation I didn't need to be in on. So I distanced myself and eavesdropped while pretending to read one of my books the teachers had allowed me to bring home for the summer. And what I heard made up for the guilt I felt for listening in.

"I know Molly May needs toys and things, especially when another child comes to play," Daddy said while cutting two similar-sized jump ropes for me. I supposed the second one was for times when Vera Lou or, I hoped, some other child might come to play.

"Well, Christmas will come before you know it," Mother replied, even though it was months before Christmas would actually arrive.

Daddy told her maybe they should sell the Hereford yearling he had bought cheap a while back and make a better Christmas. "I had intended to give that yearling a little extra grazing time at the creek bank next spring to fatten him up and then sell him for a profit," Daddy said. "But we could sure use the money now." Then they were silent, and I was pretty sure they were thinking about what they'd buy me.

Traditional Christmas hard candies weren't on my wish list. Because I craved apples, bananas, oranges, and nuts all the time, it was easy to consider *them* as Christmas treats. I also hoped Mother would make her Christmas special, chocolate layer cake, like she had back in Arkansas. Almost tasting and smelling the chocolate, I went all out and pictured myself opening my Christmas gift, a Shirley Temple doll just like the one I'd heard the well-dressed girls in my school talking about.

"Maybe there'd be enough money left after we make a better Christmas to buy a used cream separator," Daddy said to Mother, squelching my daydream of getting the famous doll in my possession. "We sure need a cream separator before we can increase our number of milk cows," he added. "And a table-model radio would be awful nice, too."

From what I could gather sitting at the kitchen table pretending to read, Mother seemed to encourage Daddy to look into buying a radio. She mentioned that one of the well-off farmers or somebody with a good, steady wage—perhaps the postmaster or the mail carrier—might trade in his table model for a floor-model radio. She also said she imagined the traded-in radio could be bought dirt cheap.

At that point my thoughts sailed back to the time when I heard Mr. Fleming tell Daddy that even after things were getting better on account of President Roosevelt's New Deal, the poor, small-scale farmers would have to wait to buy certain things. But it seemed, from what I had heard in my folks' attitude, there might be a way we could get a radio sooner and for very little money.

"Right now a radio really could ease our minds," Daddy said, picking up the subject of the radio again. Then he continued to tell Mother that he pictured the three of us gathered around the radio listening to President Roosevelt's Sunday fireside chats or to a Joe Louis boxing match, because he would soon be fighting for the world championship. I liked Mr. Roosevelt and Joe Louis, and I think Mother did, too.

"Now, Elsa Ruth, imagine a toe-tapping hoedown coming on the radio and you and me having ourselves a little jig," Daddy put in with a slight grin.

"Uh-huh," Mother said. "Or the three of us could listen to that funny show, *Amos and Andy*, or the singing show called *The Grand Old Opry*."

It sure seemed like my parents were considering a radio. I was so excited!

~

Not long after that, the yearling was attacked in the night and devoured by coyotes or a pack of wild dogs. We'd never know whether it was coyotes or dogs, and it sure didn't matter.

The yearling was gone, and so was our hope for a radio anytime soon.

What stuck in my mind most was Daddy's bursting through the kitchen door and telling us about the yearling. After he had spilled the bad news, he looked like he was going to bawl like a baby. Instead he cursed for about a straight minute, mixing in his own made-up cuss words, so as not to repeat himself, I supposed. Not that it made me feel better, but I sensed swearing was just another way for Daddy to deal with his disappointment and anger. I looked at Mother to see how she reacted, and it seemed like she was praying for Daddy quietly to herself. That was usually her way of handling her own stress, as well as coping with Daddy's outbursts.

Later that morning, when Daddy came into the house after milking the cows, he appeared quiet and embarrassed. He eased down on a kitchen chair and confessed, "I was wrong to count my chickens before they'd hatched. I was foolish wanting to spend money like I'd soon turn a corner and be rich."

Mother sat down quietly and seemed to want to have a conversation, but Daddy said no more after his confession. Mother quickly tried to cheer him up with the news that she'd have enough saved from selling eggs to buy new school shoes for me by the time school started. He looked relieved the subject had changed. Mother looked relieved, too, and then reminded him that she had just finished my new school dress and *two* matching bloomers.

"Mrs. Drecker gave me her flour sacks because all her grandchildren are boys," she proudly informed him, and he nodded appreciation for her effort. I certainly was happy to have the extra bloomers so I wouldn't have to hand-wash them as often and then worry about them drying by the morning.

When Daddy left the room, Mother leaned close to me and said, "You'll need to be more careful with your new shoes than you've been in the past, Molly May. Just walk. Don't hop, skip, or do those flying leaps like a jackrabbit escaping a wild dog's jaws."

I didn't want to remind her that she always bought my shoes way too big so I wouldn't outgrow them quickly. But they were so big for me that I scuffed them all the time on table legs, chair legs, and such. I also didn't tell her I turned my running jumps into high leaps because leaping up high with my feet not touching the ground for a good spell made me feel less sad about things—like Lettie Ruth leaving us. I often wished Daddy could leap like that so he wouldn't worry so much about the farm and especially not feel so sad about losing our beautiful baby.

~

On the first day of school that fall, my fourth-grade teacher, Miss Woods, announced, "We have lots of good things to do between now and October 1st, when school dismisses for two weeks for cotton picking."

Because it was exciting to be in the clean two-story brick building, I didn't like the idea that we'd have a break for cotton picking so soon after we just got started. But that's just how it was, and I knew I had to accept it.

For me, the large indoor toilets, one on the first floor and another on the second, were the best features of the building. It really relieved my mind to know I wouldn't need to go to an outside toilet in a dust storm.

At recess, several third- and fourth-grade girls were standing around in the first-floor girls' sparkling clean indoor restroom talking about a Shirley Temple movie they'd seen during the summer at the Westin Theater. One girl, named Thelma Lynn, sister to Mary Sue, looked more like a doll than a schoolgirl in her store-bought blue dress and her matching lace-trimmed blue socks. She had a head full of curls with a pretty blue bow amid them. When someone told her that her dress and hairstyle were very pretty, she exclaimed, "My cousin in Oklahoma City—she's my age—said that before long all young girls are going to look like Shirley Temple. I mean their hair, their clothes. Why, my cousin says even the new Morton salt girl looks like Shirley Temple." That's what I had thought in second grade, but I felt sure I should keep that thought to myself in this situation.

I wondered why Thelma Lynn couldn't wear her clothes and hair with a little less fussing. Her sister, Mary Sue, seemed low-key about her looks, most of the time. In my opinion, Thelma Lynn definitely needed to wear herself better, as I had heard Mother say about a prettily dressed teenager we'd once seen calling attention to herself in the Thistleway drugstore.

During Thelma Lynn's center-stage performance, my eyes met those of Wanda May, a girl in a new flour sack dress, whose desk was next to mine in class. She was holding a brand-new red-and-green jump rope, and she quietly asked, "Would you like to go outside and jump rope? I'll take turns letting you jump my rope, if you didn't bring yours."

"I don't have a real jump rope. Just one my daddy made with a piece of new calf rope he bought especially for that purpose, and I wouldn't bring *that* to school," I replied, quite uncomfortable for my burst of overexplaining. But Wanda May didn't seem to notice, and she suggested we go outside where it was less crowded and jump rope on the sidewalk. On the way out she confided that her older sister had married a young fellow who was making a lot of money—thirty dollars a month—working as a janitor at the county courthouse in Westin. So her sister bought her the jump rope for her birthday just a few days before school started.

Outside, two prettily dressed fourth-grade girls were talking with reasonable excitement about Shirley Temple's new movie, *Bright Eyes*. After that, they jumped rope in rhythm while singing her song "On the Good Ship Lollipop." Soon half the girls in school, it seemed, were gathered around, tapping their feet to the tune. I did, too, in my mind.

But soon Wanda May and I joined the boys on the Giant Stride, a tall structure that looked something like a huge Maypole. But the Giant Stride was all metal and had bar-shaped metal handles attached to the ends of long, sturdy chains extending from a metal disk at the top of the pole. Each of us gripped a handle, and then all of us ran around in a circle until we gained so much speed that our feet were lifted off the ground. Quickly then, we pumped our bodies and legs so vigorously that we became a circle of children flying high off the ground, as if we were chasing each other like birds in midair.

It was the most fun I'd ever had, especially since Frederick was right across from me. But I didn't let him catch me looking at him—not once, after I first noticed him anyway. Not looking at him wasn't easy. Since we were no longer in the same class, I missed seeing him every day.

Fourth-grade schoolwork was fun, though. For example, the teacher announced that every fourth-grader should write a story for the county writing contest, and it would be due the day before school was dismissed for cotton picking. The best essay would be published in the Westin newspaper. I began working on mine right away.

During the weeks before school closed for cotton picking, I

also read several fifth-grade library books on the school bus and at home. It felt good to read more grown-up books and to be in fourth grade with children who were as tall as I was. Well, some were anyway.

One girl, Estella Ann, was even taller than I, and I could tell we would become friends. She liked school as much as Wanda May and I did, and if she could learn to ride the Giant Stride as well as Wanda May and I could, there might be three girls who could ride as well as the boys. Not that I hadn't been a little afraid of playing on it after I heard Miss Woods say, "That Giant Stride is going to get another student hurt pretty bad one of these days." What a disappointment it was to hear that news. My coming from a bare-yard home with no toys or games inside made every piece of the school playground equipment a treasure to me.

~

Three days before the two-week recess for cotton picking, Miss Woods's Giant Stride prediction of disaster became a reality for me. I lost my grip on the handle while flying high off the ground, and I sailed through the air across the playground several feet before I skidded facedown across its graveled surface. My first thought was how glad I was Frederick hadn't been around to see me looking so awkward.

Miraculously, I had held my head high during the landing, and the only facial injury I had was a cut just beneath the tip of my chin. The palms of my hands and the underside of my forearms were bleeding and bruised. So were my elbows, my knees, and my pride. But fortunately I had no broken bones.

I returned to school the next morning with my purple chin swollen as big as Popeye the Sailor Man's. Everyone seemed to be standing in line to get a better look at my injuries and to pass the word to me that Miss Woods had done some investigating and contacted every member of the school board, hoping to effect some change. It turned out I was the sixth student to lose his or her grip and land on the graveled playground since the Giant Stride's installation three years before. Word was, the Giant Stride would soon be history.

~

"Howdy there, Miss Priss Molly May," said a voice I had not forgotten.

It came from the cow lot next to our barn as I was passing by, glad the long walk from the school bus was almost done. I was relieved in a way that I wouldn't have any more days of school until after cotton picking was over and my injuries had healed. It had been an unusually warm autumn day, and my not feeling top-notch good had made it feel even warmer. I wanted only to get into the house and change from my new flour sack dress into something old and comfortable. I craved quiet time. And I thought, *Please let the voice I heard be just a bad dream.*

"Didn't you go to school today?" I finally asked, once I accepted that the voice I'd heard was real.

"Yea-ah, but this is duh last day of school afore cotton picken, jest like it is ova in yer school," answered Vera Lou.

"What are you doing here, though?" I asked, in not too friendly a manner. Much to my chagrin she explained she was spending cotton-picking time with her grandparents. Instead of riding on her usual school bus to her home, she had taken the bus that went by my house; and since her grandmother was visiting my mother, she'd asked the driver to drop her off at our place.

"Is she still in our house?" I asked, worried Vera Lou would stay the rest of the afternoon—if indeed her grandmother *was* in our house.

"No, she ain't. I jest wanted tuh see how yuh look afta yer axe ta dent afore I walk on up tuh Grammar's house," she answered while stroking a calf's neck none too gently, and I recalled how cruel she had been to Hattie, the collie on Mr. and Mrs. Williams's farm, the first time that I met her.

I was glad no one was touching me roughly. I still felt sore and stiff all over, especially my back, and the cuts on the palms of my bandaged hands were wearing on my patience, and so was Vera Lou.

"How do you know about my accident?" I asked.

"Grammar told me ova da phone," she said. "Yer chin look like itsa been through da sausage grinder."

"Well," I said, changing the subject, "I have to go in the house and change my dress and help my mother."

"No, wait. Lookie here at this here long, rusty nail I found in yer cow lot. Rusty nail's a dangerous thang ifen yuh step on one barefoot. Here, yuh wont tuh put it in da trash?"

"Okay," I said, reaching for the nail and thinking maybe she'd changed a little since the last time I had seen her.

But before I knew what was happening, she grabbed the hem of my dress with one hand and stretched it out flat as a bedsheet toward her. And before I could pull the dress back, she jabbed a hole in my skirt with the nail and then ripped a long, three-cornered, four-inch tear in the middle of it. My new flour sack dress!

Pure fury flashed through me, and with my bandaged right fist I brought an uppercut to her chin—just like Daddy had shown me one time when we were talking about a Joe Louis fight. Her head flopped back, and she stumbled two steps backward and landed flat on a fresh cow pie, as we called them. She lay there looking hazy-eyed. At first I thought maybe I'd hurt her badly. But a flashback came to me of her pretended fit on our barn roof, and for a moment I thought maybe I shouldn't wait around. But I stood my ground anyway and didn't run away. Without saying a word she finally stood up, shakily I thought—I hoped. Surprisingly, she took off, and the last I saw of her, she was racing toward her grandparents' place, her backside coated in a cow's digested meal, her right hand holding her jaw.

I turned and walked toward my house, with my left hand holding my throbbing right hand, which, I thought, was beginning to swell.

"What in the world was going on between you and Vera Lou in the cow lot? All I saw was her lying on the ground and then jumping up and running away. And what was she doing here?" Mother questioned as I came through the door.

I decided to put some of the burden on Mother, and while she treated my painful right hand, I gave her the whole story about my first and this latest encounter with Vera Lou. When I finished telling her everything, Mother said, "Mrs. Williams is well aware of Vera Lou's speech and behavior problems."

Mother went on to explain that Mrs. Williams had told her just the day before that Vera Lou and her mother were, within a few days, moving permanently to the south where Vera Lou's other grandparents lived. Then Mother explained, "Their son is adjusting to the departure of his wife and stepdaughter."

"Stepdaughter," I interjected.

"Yes, stepdaughter. I hadn't known either until yesterday. It's all kind of sad. The grandparents had given up farming here when the drought and dust storms first got bad, and they returned to the south."

I felt a wave of pity for Vera Lou—until I thought about my ruined new dress.

Mother mended the dress that night, and as she handed it back to me, she said, "I hope this dress stays nice-looking enough until we can collect more flour sacks to make you a new one."

I knew I would have to wear the dress many times after that. I also knew I would never wear it without noticing the mended tear right in the front of the skirt, and regret my lapse in judgment the day I'd allowed its ruin.

Ruin! I hadn't liked that word, and that night in bed I allowed my thoughts to wander back to the words *believe* and *hope*. For a year, those words had spun through my head when I tried to cancel out my uneasiness about our struggles in our section of the world. I also wondered if I'd ever have friends who would respect me. Mother and the neighbor ladies had respectful friendships. Daddy had good friends, too.

I let my mind stray some more and recalled that it had been only a few days after Lettie Ruth died when Mr. Curtis formed the habit of stopping by for a chat with Daddy on Sunday afternoons. He was a very successful farmer of hundreds of acres of fine farmland about six miles south of us. During one of his visits I heard him say, "Tillman, one of my part-time grain harvest workers tells me he's heading for California right after this harvest. And what I'm wondering is if you would be interested in taking his job next summer. As you know, I also cut grain for several farmers who don't have their own combines."

"Well," Daddy had answered, glancing at Mother, "I'd sure like to, but I don't see how I could, what with all I got on my hands here. And I don't have a car or any means fast enough to get down to your place so I could work for you. What kind of hours are you thinking of, by the way?"

"It's at night, driving my tractor that's pulling a combine. I'm getting too old to work such long hours. I have a day crew and a night crew, you see. The tractor has battery-powered lights on it, so the hours are from six to about 10 or 11 p.m. And grain harvesting will be over by your cotton-picking time."

It turned out our neighbor Mr. Gwen also worked on the night crew, and he had told Mr. Curtis that Daddy could ride to and from the job with him. But the clincher in the deal was that Mr. Curtis would loan his tractor to Daddy to pull his wagonloads of cotton to the gin—starting this very fall. After Mr. Curtis left, Mother said his offer was a miracle and that she would help with the evening milking so Daddy could take the job.

My mental review of the good deeds that had happened between Mother and Daddy and their friends had been reassuring. I felt like I wanted to believe and hope again. So I promised myself I'd do something nice for another girl and that we might help each other to have a better life—and be friends. After all, Mother was a kind younger friend to her neighbors, and Mr. Curtis had done something good for Daddy, and Daddy could help him a lot, too.

Suddenly I was reminded of my first day in second grade when I was walking behind a girl as we exited the outdoor toilet. Her skirt in the back had been caught up in the elastic waist of her bloomers, and I hadn't whispered the problem to her, because I was too shy. If I had told her about it, she wouldn't have suffered the awful embarrassment of some students' subdued but audible snickers and comments when we returned to the playground.

I concluded that the girl and I probably would have become friends had I helped her avoid that humiliation. Then fortunately, for once, I was able to put aside my usual compulsion to worry about what might have been, and I rolled over to get the sleep I needed for the next day in the cotton field.

~

The next morning I felt less bitter about my mended new dress. But as Daddy and I walked to the field, I realized I hadn't yet conquered my bad attitude toward picking cotton. I was thinking that with my hands still sore, time would drag there. I would sweat a lot from the long sleeves and gloves I would need to wear in order to avoid scratches and punctures from the sharp bolls. I would sweat under the sunbonnet, too. But after a while I reminded myself that I had good reasons for wanting to be of good cheer. In two weeks I would be healed, and I would be back in school finding out how I did in the writing contest. But the best reason to be happy would be right here in my home.

While I was bent over picking cotton, my mind traveled back to this morning's breakfast, when I learned that a happy event would occur in our home around April 14 of the coming year.

"Only four months after our calendar for 1935 replaces the old one," Daddy had said.

"You're going to have a new baby brother or sister," Mother had chimed in, repeating her announcement made just seconds before.

Then she promised that when the new calendar arrived, she and I would circle the entire first two weeks in April. "Just in case the baby should come early," she had added with a smile.

~

After one hour in the field, I could understand the doctor's warning that Mother should not pick cotton. Pulling the heavy sacks would put her at risk of a miscarriage. I recalled that Lettie Ruth had been born a month early, the day after the razor accident when Mother had carried me on her back. I couldn't help making the connection. More worry.

My back hurt when I picked cotton, and I was only a child, but it was worth any discomfort I might experience in order to keep Mother out of the field. Although I couldn't help wishing we could afford to hire our cotton picked, like Mr. Bridges and a few other farmers did. But then after that first day in the field, it was as though I had rubbed Aladdin's lamp. After supper, a miracle happened.

~

When Mother and I finished the supper dishes, I settled down in the sitting room with a pillow at my back. In no time I was absorbed in Robinson Crusoe's life on a beautiful tropical island after having been shipwrecked there for a very long time. But I was jarred back to dry land when a knock at the front door caused me to jump and choke out, "Daddy, someone's at the door."

The sudden knocking turned out to be the Gypsies! We hadn't seen them since back in March when they hailed Daddy to stop along the road as he was coming home from Thistleway. There actually hadn't been an emergency that time in March; they simply had wanted to trade, with no money to boot, two of their fine horses for Daddy's two less strong, less muscular team. The deal had depended on Daddy's allowing them to camp for a week in our pasture, fish in our section of the creek, and hunt quail and rabbits. We never asked how they knew about our pasture or the creek.

I also remembered that they had needed to camp out with us because their caravan of Gypsies had rejected them for a violation of Gypsy rules. But it had been a false charge, and that would soon be proved. Still, they couldn't rejoin the caravan until a Gypsy trial had cleared them.

Unlike many people, Daddy didn't mistrust Gypsies in general, and that was why he agreed to the deal and loaned them two of his oldest guns, but not those that had been his grandfather's. He wished them good luck with the hunting and the unusually warm weather for March, too.

All that had been months ago, and I didn't understand why they had returned. But I figured I needed to get some sleep, and I trudged off to bed thinking I'd wait until morning to find out from Daddy why the Gypsies were back.

~

"I was relieved the Gypsies hadn't come to reclaim their gentle, hardworking horses," admitted Daddy the next morning at breakfast when he told us about the second good deal he'd made with our night callers.

The large extended family had arrived two weeks ahead of the time they were supposed to be in our area in order to rejoin their larger caravan for the trial. Once the charges were dropped, they would officially rejoin the caravan on its way to Arizona to work in carnivals, and then on to California. So the senior member proposed that his group harvest our cotton, if they could again set up camp in our pasture with the same privileges as before.

Although Gypsies were not known to be migrant cotton pickers, Daddy agreed to their proposal and allowed them to set up camp. Then he dug out all the cotton sacks he had brought all the way from Arkansas, which Grandpa Dryden had given us when he retired from farming. And, once again, the Gypsies stationed their colorfully painted wagons next to the well in our pasture.

I couldn't believe my luck! That might mean less time in the field for me, and I wouldn't need to carry water, either. The Gypsies insisted they would carry well water to our house twice a day. Their presence was also a source of entertainment during our balmy fall nights. At dusk we could hear and see them when they cooked their wild game—mostly rabbits—outside on a campfire and later when they played their instruments, sang, and danced.

I couldn't have been prouder of my daddy when Mr. Williams and others commented on his good deal with the Gypsies, and Daddy responded, "I don't think they'll catch many fish, but there are plenty of rabbits and probably enough quail for our table, and theirs. And, well, they don't leave any clutter around, or steal from me or my neighbors."

I felt then and still do that Mr. Williams and the others understood Daddy's generosity toward the Gypsies. Mr. and Mrs. Williams and the other equally kind neighbors had given us a helping hand when we needed it. We likely weren't the first, or the last, to be on the receiving end of such kindness during Oklahoma's worst of times.

~

When I took notice of Mr. Curtis's tractor leaving our field with the wagonload of cotton hitched to the back of it, I felt good. I couldn't imagine how a tenant farmer without a tractor could pull his cotton to the gin with horses and be back in time to do any picking. Still, it ate up a good portion of a day for Daddy to take a wagon of cotton to the gin with a tractor that could go three times as fast as our team of strong horses. It turned out Daddy could at times be absent from the field for several hours because there was a long line of farmers waiting to unload their cotton. Meanwhile, the Gypsies had to empty their sacks of picked cotton on a large canvas tarp Mr. Curtis had loaned to Daddy for that purpose.

Mother had already decided I shouldn't work in the field while Daddy was away. I felt my ears flutter with interest when I heard her say to Daddy, "It wouldn't be right to leave Molly May in the cotton field and expect the Gypsies to weigh and empty her cotton sack and watch after her."

"Why not? She doesn't need to be watched, does she?" asked Daddy.

"Because she might feel self-conscious around the boys," Mother answered, a little crisply for her. "Remember, they're older than she is."

She was right. I might. I didn't really think the Gypsy boys would make me feel uncomfortable, but I understood her worry. I'd not been comfortable on the school bus or on the school grounds when I couldn't help overhearing the older boys say things I didn't care to hear. But regardless of what the reasons were for taking me out of the cotton field, I had to restrain myself from doing a gleeful squeak at the thought of being excused from the hard work—at least for part of a day.

I also learned that during my time off from the field, another bonus would fall in my lap. I heard Mother say to Daddy, "I invited the smaller Gypsy girls to come to our house to play with Molly May. They're too young to do anything but trudge beside their mothers in the field or sit in the shade of the wagon. With the wagon not there, they have no shade. So the little girls can come here every time you're hauling cotton to the gin."

It certainly was a bonus when the girls brought dolls their mothers had made and groomed in handcrafted, brightly colored dresses with beautifully embroidered accents. They told me their mothers and grandmothers sold the dolls and doll clothing at carnivals, as well as baskets they had woven and a number of other items. They taught me Gypsy children's songs in a strange language, too. I could hardly wait for school to start again so I could tell my best friends, Wanda May and Estella Ann, about the songs, dolls, and doll dresses. Estella Ann was a farm girl, too, and would appreciate my story about our unusual and interesting workers during cotton-picking time.

~

When school recess for cotton picking ended, it felt like school resumed more quickly than I had imagined. While waiting for the starting bell to ring, Miss Woods overheard me telling my two best friends about the Gypsies, and she asked me if I would take about five minutes of first period to tell the class about them. I surprised myself and said I would, and I surprised myself even more when I didn't get terribly shy while telling my story in front of the whole class.

Later that same day Miss Woods announced, "Molly May did exceptionally well in the county writing contest."

I couldn't help noticing that even those who hadn't been very interested in entering the contest sat up straighter in their seats. Others looked at me with way-to-go smiles.

"Her topic," continued Miss Woods, "was 'An Event I'll Never Forget,' and she won first prize. Let me also remind you that her essay will be published in the *Westin Weekly* next week. But before you come up for your prize, Molly May, tell the class a little about your topic."

For the second time that day I stood next to my desk like I

was supposed to and told the class that my essay was about my family's first dust storm experience stranded with some other people in a small cafe, and that it was the first time I had ever seen a centipede. When I sat down, one boy in my class said, "I got bit by a centipede once, too, and I was sicker than a dog, and the flesh around the bite rotted and came right off. Here, look at the scar." Some of the girls said *ew-w-w,* while most of the boys gawked at where the boy had pulled his pant leg up to reveal the scar just above his ankle.

The teacher thanked the boy for sharing and then asked the class if there were any more stories about the critters that had been brought on so abundantly by the drought and dust. One student told about his spider bite, and a girl told about a scorpion's sting on her big toe.

"Well," said Miss Woods, stepping nearer the front and center of the room when the girl had finished her story, "it seems like we're full of interesting stories today, and it's good to hear that you handled your injuries so well. You were very brave, I'm sure. Thank you very much, students. And now, Molly May, please come forward for your prize."

I felt sorry that I was the only one getting a reward. I happened to know there were honorable mentions in that contest, and I was sure at least two of my classmates had written as well as I had, and they should have been given prizes, too. But when I saw my prize for three dollars, I was impressed by the large amount and my name on the check. For a second I felt more rich than famous.

But I didn't feel rich for very long before I heard Mother's voice telling me I had better save my prize money for when I would need the next new pair of shoes. *I can do that*, I thought. I had seen nice girls' shoes in the sale catalog for $1.49 and once on a store sale table for quite a bit less. Then I thought about the winter sniffle season coming up and having to use a rag instead of a handkerchief like the better-dressed girls in school used. I recalled having seen boxes of ten handkerchiefs for 99 cents in the dime store, and I did the math. If I splurged for the box of ten handkerchiefs, I would still have a lot of money to save for new shoes the next time I would need them, as well as enough to buy Wanda May a nickel ice cream cone a couple of times when I had one. Yes, I definitely would buy the handkerchiefs, which would be both a luxury and a necessity, since Kleenex was unheard of in our part of the world.

~

Shortly after my first day back in school, Daddy surprised us and came home from Thistleway with a used icebox. Mr. Elkhart at the hardware store had given it to Daddy because he no longer had space for it and was looking for someone to take it off his hands.

It was a good-looking, varnished icebox in solid oak with gold-covered metal handles and hinges. We thought it must have come from the richest home in the whole county.

"Let's buy ice right away and keep this handsome piece of furniture in our kitchen until the weather gets really cold and we put it on the porch," Mother said, polishing the handle with the hem of her apron.

"O-h-h-h, why can't we keep it in the house all the time?" I nagged. "It looks so pretty."

Mother agreed that it looked fine as could be in our house, but for the winter we would put it on the back porch, where a fifty-pound block of ice would last for a very long time. That way, eggs, milk, and cream would be kept cold without much cost.

She assured me the icebox would be back in the kitchen the first warm day of spring.

"Imagine, Molly Girl, in summer we'll have ice, and we'll be drinking cold milk," Mother said excitedly, "and maybe we can have Kool-Aid or lemonade for the Fourth of July or some other special day."

I questioned how we would be able to afford the ice so often during the summer; Mother just shook her head as if to shut out my negative thought, and she said, "We'll find a way to pay for a chunk of ice every few days."

I tried to fight off my doubt.

"Look how the Gypsies' labor in the cotton field didn't cost us anything." Mother glowed, squelching my doubtfulness a little. "And how your daddy will be earning some money working nights for Mr. Curtis's next wheat harvest. And also remember, because your daddy agreed to work long, hard hours, we were able to use Mr. Curtis's tractor to haul our cotton to the gin. Yes, we'll find a way. We always do."

I glanced at Daddy to see if he was as doubtful as I still was. But he seemed to agree with Mother. "Yep, the cotton harvest turned out okay, and I was able to put some money in the bank," said Daddy, which relaxed my mind—a little anyway.

"It'll go toward the cost of a truck. That is, if we find one at the right price," said Mother.

But I said to myself, *We'll need to buy feed for the spring chickens and cotton seed for next year's crop. There's no end to the number of things we'll need.* I hated to worry like that, but sometimes when my folks seemed a bit too optimistic, I couldn't help it.

I hoped having a little extra money meant there would be enough to buy Christmas nuts, apples, oranges, and bananas to last a couple of days.

In Arkansas we had gathered around the potbellied stove on Christmas Eve and Christmas night, and I loved that. We cracked walnuts and ate their kernels along with slices of fruit. Our Arkansas Christmases were definitely more festive than the one we had when we lived in the shanty. And much had happened since then. So I wanted to tuck the most sorrowful and scary times into the very back of my mind. It seemed Mother and Daddy wanted to do that, too, and I needed to follow suit.

~

Christmas! I had decided a long while back what gifts I'd buy for my folks. It happened one day when Wanda May invited Estella Ann and me to come to her house and eat our home-packed lunches during lunch break while she ate at home. She wanted to stop in at the dime store on our way, and I was disappointed she wanted to stop there. I was looking forward to eating my lunch at the same table with Wanda May's twin brother, Jeremy. Not that he ever talked to me when I was there, or at school. Since other boys at school *did* talk to me without my help, I left it up to him to start a conversation. In a nutshell, I knew I was still a child, and I wouldn't allow myself to be noticeably boy crazy like some older girls on the school bus seemed to be.

But I tagged along into the store and saw a very bright red bandanna handkerchief for Daddy and a tiny lace-trimmed white handkerchief for Mother. "More for show than blow," as the nice clerk who showed it to me had said. Right then, I made up my mind to buy the bandanna and the dainty handkerchief as soon as I could earn enough money.

Over the next few weeks I did indeed earn the money doing chores for Mr. Owens at the gas station. I'd arrive at the station earlier on cold mornings, hoping he'd have chores for me to do when I came inside to stay warm until the school bus arrived. I also hoped he hadn't figured out I was arriving earlier just to get the work. But I have to say there was always plenty to do. There were dirty dishes and fruit jars, ashes on the floor around the heating stove, wastepaper baskets running over, pop cooler and candy cases only half-filled, and so on.

I worked hard and fast to get the work done before the school bus came, and I would finish in the afternoon what I didn't get done in the morning. Walking home later in the day, I allowed myself to feel good about my hard work rather than worry that Mr. Owens really didn't want or maybe even think he needed my help. I figured I deserved a reward for something I had worked hard for, just like I had when I won the essay-writing contest.

~

I applied a similar logic to the fact that Daddy had continued to accept some benefits of President Roosevelt's New Deal.

At the supper table one night Daddy explained that if all farmers plowed up portions of their cotton fields, there would be a shortage of cotton, and cotton prices would go up.

He had accepted this point of view because his family's needs counted more than his nitpicking at the politics. He knew there was coal to be bought for cooking and heating. And there would be the doctor's bill for delivering the baby in the coming spring. Daddy detested debt. Pride was a key element in his determination, his perseverance.

~

I was disappointed when it seemed like we'd have very little money for Christmas. I imagined that we'd have the skimpiest Christmas of any small-scale farmer. An increased number of other farmers in our area took part-time jobs with the Works Progress Administration, known as WPA, building or repairing roads and doing other projects. I'd heard children in school say they wouldn't have had this or that if their daddies hadn't been hired to work on WPA projects. But Daddy refused that kind of work. There were times I wished Daddy would swallow his pride. We sure could have used the money, especially if he could work during the winter.

~

It had been a long time since I'd heard Mother singing in the kitchen. But I heard her singing on December 24 while she was going all out making a Christmas cake. It turned out to be a masterpiece, a three-layer chocolate cake covered in chocolate-fudge frosting with pecan halves embedded in the icing and arranged in the shape of Christmas trees.

"Hail to the best of chocolate cake bakers!" I said in as castle-like a voice as I could muster when the final pecan Christmas tree was in place on the creamy fudge frosting. Mother laughed and said, "Oh, Molly May Dowden, stop talking like that. You've read too many fairy tale books in your day."

~

My folks' budget made buying an evergreen Christmas tree impossible, so Daddy walked to the creek and cut the top off a scrubby sapling to improvise as our holiday tree for that year.

Mother and I made red and green construction-paper chains to drape around it. Even I could see the tree was quite pathetic, with its yellow leaves barely clinging to twiggy branches that were hardly strong enough to hold up the paper decoration. But we pretended it was a great Christmas tree, and that's all that mattered.

Mother's delicious chicken and dumpling soup was a lip-smacking good Christmas Eve supper. After we had eaten the soup, we opened our Christmas gifts next to our potbellied stove in the sitting room. My gifts to my parents went over very big. And I received a cereal bowl with Shirley Temple's picture on it and a skinny-legged rag doll with short, straight black hair from Mother and Daddy. There also was the usual pair of colorful knee-high socks from Maribelle—which I loved—and a quarter from Grandpa and Grandma Dryden. Poor Grandpa and Grandma. "They've been spending a lot of their money on doctor bills and medicines," Mother said. "Your grandma's even been in the hospital a couple of times." On hearing that, I hoped they wouldn't run out of money before it was time for them to die.

"The cereal bowl came free in a box of Wheaties, and we'll eat the cereal for Christmas breakfast," Mother explained. "We wanted you to have a Shirley Temple doll, but—"

"This doll is fine," I interrupted, and close to outright lying, I added, "She's famous, too. See, she looks like Olive Oyl, Popeye's girlfriend. I like her."

After that, we cracked and ate a few peanuts, some pecans, and three Brazil nuts, which tasted exactly like the coconut Mrs. Bridges had let me taste once when she was making a pie. When we finished off the nuts, we each peeled and ate a large, sweet orange. All that good eating was just a prelude to Christmas Day, when we had oven-baked chicken with corn bread dressing, three vegetables, and of course, the chocolate cake! The leftovers lasted for two more days, and I felt like a well-fed princess.

~

When school resumed after Christmas, Miss Woods informed the class that I had spelled every single word correctly on a qualifying test for the county spelling contest we had all taken before the Christmas break. I would be going to the county spelling test in Westin in April.

I was both surprised and pleased, not to mention determined to memorize hundreds of words that might help me win the contest. But soon I began to worry, and I confessed to Miss Woods that I wasn't a natural speller. She simply laughed, shook her head, and said, "Oh, Molly May, don't underestimate yourself. Come to my desk when the dismissal bell rings at four o'clock, and I'll give you a list of words to memorize—hundreds of them!"

For the next several days I often pictured myself in Westin representing my class. Even during lunchtime, I sometimes thought about the spelling contest, especially when I wanted to tune out the girls who had received Shirley Temple dolls for Christmas. I wanted to feel as important and happy as they did, and I had high hopes that winning the Westin contest in the spring would accomplish that for me.

Chapter Four

By the time we turned our calendar to March of 1935, frequent dust storms that continued into the night hindered my efforts to study the spelling contest words Miss Woods had given me, or to get a decent night's sleep.

I was worried about Mother, too. The whites of her eyes had become so red they looked like balls of blood, and her irises could hardly be seen, except from close up. Light was so painful to her eyes that the doctor told her she'd need to lie down in a darkened room with a damp washcloth folded thick over her eyes until a dust storm had moved on. Time ticked slowly for her during that series of storms, and at times she grew impatient, and she'd break enough to complain just a little.

"I do nothing but follow doctor's orders," she once lamented. "I'm putting drops in my eyes three times a day, taking aspirin every few hours for the pain and inflammation—all just little things, and only for myself. Your daddy and you are doing all the housekeeping, cooking, and looking after me."

Truthfully, I allowed Daddy to do most of Mother's bedside care. He seemed to need to feed her and make sure she had remembered to use her eye drops and take her aspirin, and he placed near her all that she needed for washing, brushing her teeth, and combing her hair.

Mother *was* a pitiful sight, with her face concealed in cloth and her stomach a very noticeable mound. I imagined Daddy and I weren't an appealing-looking pair either, with a red bandanna handkerchief tied over his face and my face covered with a rag mask, which muffled our coughs and voices. When we had to wear masks in school and on the school bus, some kids would pretend once in a while to be bank robbers. The rest of us laughed at them. Sometimes we all simply needed to make light of things. But at home it wasn't always so easy to look at the lighter side.

Daddy and I had to clean our eyes often because the dust collected in the rims of our eyes and in our lashes. We looked like opossums. I wanted to joke about our funny-looking eyes, but with all the day-after-day storms, I couldn't quite squelch my attitude toward our home circumstances enough to laugh. Remembering how we had giggled on the school bus about the masks, I wished I could have laughed for Daddy's sake.

"Dust is everywhere. It gets in our food, makes it hard to sleep, and intrudes on our bodies," I said in disgust to Daddy one morning, sounding so much like Mother it startled me. He must have been startled, too, because he just looked at me.

~

After the back-to-back dust storms of early March moved on, we looked forward to summer with hope the dust storms wouldn't return and that the summer would not be suffocatingly hot. With the decrease in the number of storms, Mother's eye problem subsided, and the solid red in the white part of her eyes faded to a marbled pink and white. She would insist that she help clean up the everyday fallout of dust that seemed to come from curtains, walls, and everywhere else. Unfortunately, there was an increase in house dust when an aptly named *dust devil* would play its dirty trick. It would look as though it were going to miss our house by several feet, and then it would take a sudden turn and make a direct hit before we could close the open windows and doors.

Mother's eyes seemed only slightly irritated from cleaning the house, but we insisted she limit herself to just the cooking. We finally won out, and it was uplifting to have her in charge of the meals again, especially since she was so optimistic that she was over her eye problem forever. That was her typical reaction whenever her eyes improved after every lull in the storms.

But there was no extended relief from dust storms in early April. Again, Mother was forced to go back to the darkened room and cover her eyes. That, and the eye drops and aspirin, were the only known means for relieving her *iritis*, as the doctor called it. History later recorded it as *dust eye*. With every episode of her iritis, Daddy and I, coughing and tired, resumed our caregiving roles, while also taking care of our main jobs—provider and student, respectively.

With the increase in the number of dust storms yet again, school days were often shortened or canceled, and the farmers' chores were necessarily modified. But whenever we lost time due to the storms, we'd work twice as hard to make up for it as soon as we could. Mother, too, felt the need to make up for her lost time. The baby was almost due, and her stomach was very large. She wanted to wash Lettie Ruth's baby clothes and crib bedding, which she had stored freshly washed after the sweet baby died. Mother was sure dust had sifted into the storage boxes during the recent storms, and she wanted the items dust free and clean for the new baby.

"Who would have thought a woman couldn't wash and dry

laundry for weeks on end!" Mother said weakly one morning as the dirt-filled wind peppered the windowpanes.

~

Finally, with only a few days left before the date the doctor said the baby might arrive, the sky was dust free for a day. Mother's eyes felt better, and she was able to wash and dry the baby things outside. After she had folded them and carefully put them away, she took two of our quilts outside to the clothesline—without telling Daddy and me.

She somehow managed to flip the quilts over the clothesline without losing her balance, temporarily impaired due to her big stomach. At least to me she looked like her humongous front would cause her to fall on her face any minute just during normal chores. But she had whapped the quilts with the side of a broom only a couple of times before Daddy and I heard and ran out to her. Daddy took the broom from her and resumed the pounding, and Mother and I went into the house.

"My, oh, my," Mother said to me quietly while we watched Daddy from the kitchen window. "Would you look at the dust coming out of those quilts. Just imagine what the wash water would have looked like, if there had been enough water to wash them before the next dirty day arrives."

It was a good thing Mother had squeezed in the task of getting the baby things washed and dried and the quilts as dust free as possible. We didn't know it, but we had used up the one good day we would have before the worst dust storm in the history of the southwest would hit us.

Fortunately, Daddy had gone to Thistleway that one good day with the cream and eggs and traded them for much-needed flour, rice, and dried pinto beans. Unbeknownst to us, we were as well prepared as we could have been for what lay ahead for us.

~

April 14, 1935. I remember it well. It was a bright Sunday afternoon, and it was apparent the rest of the day would be clear and the temperature ideal. Mother's eyes were still pinkish, but as it was after every cluster of dust storms, she thought she'd seen the last of them, and her iritis, too. She began to pry out the rag strips Daddy and I had chinked into the cracks around the windows' wood sashes, which had shrunk due to the long-lasting droughts.

Since I had helped stuff those strips of rags into the window gaps while Mother lay with her eyes covered, I felt uneasy about seeing the strips removed. But then Daddy came in from gathering the eggs and relieved my mind. "It'd be ungodly if we'd get any more dust storms this spring. Looks like your Mother might be thinking that, too."

Reluctantly I helped Mother remove the strips, but after a few minutes, she suddenly stood very still and cradled her lower stomach with her hands, and a strange look came over her face.

"What's wrong?" I asked, fearing I already knew the answer.

"I think the baby will come today," she answered as calmly as she would have if she were referring to a letter she was expecting from Grandma Dryden.

Daddy set down the pan of eggs he was about to take to the icebox and rushed to Mother's side.

"Don't worry, Tillman. Remember it takes me a while," Mother assured him in a strong voice. "You have plenty of time to go to Mr. and Mrs. Williams's house and call the doctor. Thank goodness the baby is coming on such a beautiful day."

"I'm going to ride Nellie up there. Nellie's not terrible fast, but she can get there quicker than I could run it," Daddy said as he grabbed his work hat and headed to the barn to put Nellie in the rein and bit. Nellie was the faster and smarter of our two workhorses. I told myself to relax.

Daddy was scarcely on the road before Mother told me where to find all the things that would be needed for the baby's arrival and to put them on one side of the bed in the sitting room where the baby would be born. Meanwhile, she paced back and forth between the sitting room and the kitchen.

During one of her treks to the kitchen, she looked out the window and loudly called out, "Lord have mercy, come look at this!"

I rushed to the window and looked out, and in the distance I saw a huge curtain of the darkest dirt I'd ever seen. It seemed to reach higher in the sky than birds could fly, and it was moving along like a gigantic rolling pin flattening a mound of piecrust dough. The storm was, in fact, so wide I couldn't see the ends of it. I didn't know it at the time, but it would soon be called "the roller" and then later dubbed "Black Sunday."

"It looks to be way over a mile high," Mother said, more to herself than to me, "and it's so wide I can't even see the ends of it."

"What will happen to Daddy?" I asked, shaky-voiced.

"Don't worry. He's at least halfway back home by now. Nellie will know she must hurry," Mother said confidently.

I ran to the other window, where I could see the road better, and indeed, I spotted Daddy and Nellie homeward bound only a little way up the road, and I saw that Mother was right. Nellie was clipping along faster than I ever thought she could. But within less than a minute, I witnessed a horrible sight.

The roller engulfed them, and I could see neither the faintest blur of them nor the sun. I frantically turned to tell Mother, and I almost slammed into her stomach. She had been standing right behind me and had seen them swallowed up and the sun disappear, too. Then, before we could believe what our eyes had witnessed, it became black as midnight all around us.

The roller had struck our house, and soon we could barely see the furniture.

"Get the lantern behind the kitchen stove!" Mother called to me.

"But the lamp is right on the table. I'll light it," I said wondering what was wrong with Mother's thinking. Usually we used the lantern only in the storm cellar.

"No! Get the lantern," she spoke, raising her voice. "It won't flare up as bad as the lamp will from the drafts coming in around the windows where we've taken out the rag strips and the kitchen door, where we're removed the sheet that covered it."

I lit the lantern, coughing at the same time. With one hand we held wet rags over our faces from our eyes down while we did whatever we needed to do with the other hand. I urged Mother to lie down and pull the damp cloth over her eyes, too. She wouldn't consider it at first; she just wanted to continue pacing back and forth. Finally she agreed to lie down and allow me to put the wet rag over her eyes. And the roller—the dust storm or whatever the media later would tag it—raged on.

~

It turned out the doctor had been delivering a baby in town when Daddy called him, and he never made it to our house. But Daddy arrived home in plenty of time to put Nellie into the barn with the rest of the livestock, untie his red bandanna mask from his face, and wash the dirt from his eyes and hands before he welcomed my almost-eleven-pound baby brother, Tillman Jr., whom we would call Tilley.

When Daddy lifted Tilley to bundle him in a blanket, he said, "Well, Elsa Ruth, all the red beans, rice, and rabbit meat you ate went right to this here boy. Just look at him. He must be two feet long!"

"Yes, I guess stories of his arrival during an unbelievable dust storm and the size of him will put an interesting spin on our family stories," Mother answered weakly while watching Daddy bundle the lusty-voiced baby in the baby blanket, which she had finished only a few days before her eyes had become so painful.

Daddy snickered at Mother's comment about family stories and then began to give me instructions. "Rinse the dust out of the cover for your mother's face and put it back on her eyes and nose. Then help me fasten a dampened sheet over the crib to keep the baby from breathing the dust. After that, we'll stretch a damp sheet over our bed, and we'll put one over your bed, too. There's plenty of clothespins to fasten the sheets real good."

"But we don't have enough sheets to do that," I informed him.

"That's all right," he snapped. "We'll just have to sleep on the bare mattresses."

I've never forgotten Daddy's efficiency when he'd take the role of caregiver and homemaker. For during frightening times he certainly seemed to feel like the onus was on him for bringing his family into such severe hard times. How stressful it must have been for him to finally accept the facts—the difficult conditions were not going to phase out anytime soon. At times it truly seemed as though the drought, the dust storms, and the economic depression were fused into one entwined thing—and it was as if it were an albatross hanging around my daddy's neck. Mother had told me a story about a huge bird called an albatross that hung around a man's neck because he'd made a mistake. I didn't want my daddy to feel that kind of burden. I just wanted him to continue taking care of himself and us like he had during so many difficult times.

One thing Daddy couldn't do much about was to keep the dust out of our food long enough for us to take more than a few bites without feeling our teeth crunching dirt. It was impossible for us to eat the food faster than dust could get into it. Only Tilley, underneath the sheet canopy over the big bed, lay cradled next to Mother enjoying a dirt-free supper.

By lantern light Daddy and I could see dust was piling so high on the uncaulked windows that it cascaded off the narrow sills onto the dust-covered floor. And when Mother heard our comments about it, she raised her head, lifted her eye cover from one eye, took a peek, and said, "Like a Niagara Falls of dirt. Wish it *was* water. But let's just go to sleep for now. No sense in shoveling until it's done."

~

We certainly did shovel. By morning the dirt lay so thick on the floors, we had to shovel before we used a broom. Outside, the sky was still dirt-tinged, but the roller had moved on, leaving its dirty deeds everywhere.

Mr. and Mrs. Williams stopped by to check on us and to tell us the news they'd heard on the radio. "One announcer feller dubbed this here storm 'Black Sunday'; another was still calling it 'the roller,' just like we did when we first saw it come rolling in," Mr. Williams stated, more excited than any news reporter could ever get. "In some areas, people and animals have not fared as well as we have. Houses and farm buildings have been buried deep in dirt—some up to their roofs."

"Some grown-ups and children who were caught a little distance from home have perished in the dust," added Mrs. Williams.

"Yep," said Mr. Williams, "one eight-year-old boy from around here was with his folks visiting relatives. They's just over the Texas border someplace, and the boy, he got lost in the roller. Found dead in a drift of dirt. Can't rightly say who he was. Didn't catch his name."

"Why did he get lost? Were his folks lost, too?" I asked rapid-fire, all my shyness left behind and fearing it might be a boy I knew from school. I was disappointed that Mr. and Mrs. Williams had not heard the boy's name. I hoped they hadn't heard the news correctly, and the boy wasn't from our area at all. Or, I thought, maybe they'd been wrong about the boy's age, and maybe he was actually much older or younger. Not that I wouldn't feel sad, regardless.

~

When Daddy returned from Thistleway a day later, we heard more reports. Babies, small children, and elderly folks were near death from lungs clogged with dust; some had already died of pneumonia, and others were not expected to live. Animals trapped inside tall dunes of dirt had suffocated. People were still digging out houses; farm buildings and farm equipment were embedded in the dirt, too. Besides the tragedies and the many nuisances of digging out and cleaning up, some other unexpected situations needed folks' attention.

One of the situations that struck me most was that the extremely dry, dust-laden atmosphere had created static electricity in barbed-wire fences, cars, trucks, and tractors. So people had to attach long chains underneath their vehicles in order to prevent electric shock to anyone who touched them. And as the chains dragged on the ground, a cloud of dust rose. "Just what we need, more disgusting dust," Daddy added. "And folks don't have enough water to wash their cars. They just have to wait until the wind blows off the dust."

All of Daddy's reports held my interest, but I was eager to ask the question that was still uppermost in my mind: "Did you hear the name of the boy from Thistleway who died in the big roller storm?"

"No, no, I didn't," Daddy answered. "I forgot to ask about him what with so many stories about the storm."

That settled it in my mind. I decided for my own good that whoever he was, he probably wasn't from Thistleway. I just couldn't keep on feeling so extremely concerned about a person I might not even know. I had other things to worry about.

Within a day or two, the shock of Black Sunday eased somewhat, and some folks circulated funny stories. I never forgot this one: A man driving on a country road the day after the storm noticed a hat lying atop a tall pile of dirt, and it looked to him like a fine hat. He stopped his car, walked up to the top of the mound of dirt, and picked up the hat. He was shocked when he realized the hat had been on the head of a young man buried almost up to his nose. The driver quickly recovered and asked the young fellow if he might give him a ride. The young man answered, "No, sir, don't need a ride. I'm sittin' on my horse."

"Smiles are hard to come by," Mother said to Daddy after he had passed the tale on to her. "And tall tales like that one probably lighten our hearts for a minute or two before we get on with the aftermath."

In our house the cleaning up became more difficult for Daddy and me. We were plugging along, sick with fevers and coughs from the Black Sunday storm. Daddy wasn't stricken as badly as I was, and he never allowed himself to be sick in bed. He did, however, make mustard plasters for us to put on our chests at night.

School was dismissed for two, maybe three days following that most terrible of all dust storms. It didn't matter to me, because I was too sick for days to attend school anyway. According to the report I heard afterward, my fever was so high that I became delirious. Daddy didn't realize my condition was so serious until he stopped by my bedside to tell me he was going to the well to get water. I suddenly stood on the bed, snatched his hat from his head, pointed toward the door with wild eyes, and said, "I have to go find Daddy and Nellie out there, out there in the roller!"

The worst part about my illness was that I missed the spelling contest in Westin. Mother tried to make it easier for me when she said, "You'll qualify for that spelling contest in Westin another year."

Her words of assurance didn't help. I knew I would always study for my regular weekly spelling tests so that I'd spell every word correctly, but I would never want to memorize so many words again for a county contest. I wanted to focus on writing stories instead.

~

When I was well enough to go back to school, I heard news that made me very happy. Wanda May, who had misspelled only one word in the qualifying test we had taken months earlier, had gone to the county spelling contest in my place. She had placed second in the county. That, I thought happily, was better than I could have done, even if I had been in peak condition.

~

After dealing with the effects of the roller and the many less devastating storms that followed in the days after Black Sunday, feeling happy about very many things was an effort. I was eager to make up the work I'd missed in school while I was sick and get on with the regular schoolwork. But during my lunch period on the first day back in school, I overheard something that would make Black Sunday indelible in my mind.

"His face looked as white as milk," said one girl quietly.

"Well, I couldn't even look at him," her friend replied.

They were sitting by the door, and I happened to be sitting near them eating my lunch waiting for Wanda May to return from eating lunch at home. I hadn't intended to eavesdrop.

"I felt so sorry for Frederick's mother and daddy that I couldn't even look at him in his casket," said a third girl, glancing over at me after the word *casket* had caused me to gasp and cover my mouth with my hand.

The boy from Thistleway who had died on Black Sunday was Frederick! I stood up, took a step, and then saw the floor rising toward my face.

In an instant Miss Woods and Wanda May, who had just come through the door, were helping me to stand, and I heard someone say, "I think she tripped and fell."

I didn't deny that remark, and I hoped the story would stick. And, in an instant, the memory of the death of my dear little sister washed over me. *I will not cry, I will not cry,* waved in my mind.

Later, Wanda May told me the details: Frederick and his two cousins had been playing catch on an empty lot at the edge of a Texas border town when the roller hit. The cousins lost sight of Frederick as they all raced home. But apparently Frederick had become disoriented and strayed in the wrong direction. He was found in a drift of dirt the next morning behind an abandoned gas station near where the boys had been playing.

When I tried to tell my folks about Frederick that night, I forgot my no-crying vow. I quickly stopped crying, however, when Tilley woke up and started crying, too. I reminded myself I shouldn't cry like a baby. I needed to be strong. I had heard Mother say more than once that having strength during hard times was a must—an absolute must.

~

A couple of months after the roller and Tilley's birth, the summer became unbelievably hot and dry. To keep my attitude positive about the weather and hard times, I looked for encouraging signs that life was good, after all. For one thing, I could tell that Daddy was enjoying even more respect among the men in our area. My sense of that was confirmed when his friend Mr. Curtis came one morning and told him his oldest brother, who farmed south of Westin, had died, and his wife would be selling the farm and moving in with her daughter, who lived in town. Like most women then, she hadn't learned to drive, and she wanted to sell her husband's 1932 truck.

"It's got hardly any miles on it, and it's in excellent shape, but since she doesn't drive or even want to drive at this point, she doesn't need it," said Mr. Curtis. "And I wanted you to be the first to see the truck." Then he quoted the asking price.

"I trust your judgment. Tell her I'll take it," said Daddy without hesitation.

The next day Mr. Curtis took all four of us in his car to see his sister-in-law about her truck. It turned out the lady lived in a beautiful big home much like the Bradshaw house, and she had heart. She asked Daddy if he would like to pay for the truck in three installments: one-third down, one-third next year, and the final one-third the following year. No interest at any time. To myself, I breathed a thankful sigh for the miracle; now Daddy wouldn't have to worry so much about the money he had to spend buying cottonseed to replace a field of young cotton plants the roller had taken with it.

"Who in the heck has money these days to make payments on a truck?!" said Mr. Curtis's sister-in-law. "Even if I could get a buyer, a little dab of interest doesn't amount to a poot in a whirlwind these days. Anyways, my brother-in-law has talked a lot about what an honest, hardworking man you are."

Then, as if that wasn't enough, she added, "You can have the radio from the barn, too, if you don't already have one. My husband always listened to it while he milked the cows."

"How much are you asking for it?" Daddy asked.

I held my breath hoping she wouldn't ask for much, remembering Mother had said secondhand table models could be bought dirt cheap.

"No, no, please just take it," she insisted. "It has a brand-new battery, but the radio's old, and I have two almost-new ones in the house anyway. It's nice having my electricity-powered one in the sitting room and another in the kitchen. But I don't need any more." Then she explained that she needed to get rid of a lot of things fast, including a good but old used car. She most certainly wouldn't need the truck and the extra radio, living with her daughter in town.

~

"I guess it's easier to be kind and generous when you're not hard-pressed for money and all that it will buy," said Mother on the way home in our own gently used truck. "But I think her heart was touched when she tickled Tilley's chin and he smiled for the first time, which made us all so happy."

As we rode along, Daddy said, "Being able to buy this truck like we did, and the lady giving us the radio for free, must be a sign that things are about to turn around." Daddy's comment sounded like something Mother would say.

"Yes, well," Mother responded, "that could be called a miracle, and it was actually something like a miracle when the government paid us to slaughter our two oldest cows, which were no longer good milk producers."

Daddy agreed but added his disapproval of the government's idea that getting rid of milk cows would bring up the price of dairy products. "Look at our case. We just turned around and used some of that money to buy some extra feed so the young cows we have left will produce more milk, and before long we'll have more milk cows, too."

"I know it, and we have the truck now," responded Mother. "And we'll save time, now that we have it, taking cream to town as often as we need to. Besides," she continued, sitting a little taller, "everyone knows how dangerous it is to get caught traveling in a wagon when an unexpected dust storm hits." Such excitement from Mother about owning a truck!

The radio improved my spirits tremendously. I was looking forward to listening to the Wheaties-sponsored adventure program *Jack Armstrong, the All-American Boy.* Hearing some of the girls and boys on the playground talking about the show had made me feel left out—but not anymore.

~

With the drought and dust storms continuing well into the summer, the grass had become so scarce in our pasture that we constantly feared our cows would rip through Mr. Gwen's fence to get at his field of cane. Images came back to me of the one time when they had broken down the fence and gorged themselves—to the point that they lay moaning on the ground, bloated and in pain. One cow died.

Some of the cows' udders and teats had been cut when they broke through the barbed-wire fence, and Daddy had to treat their wounds night and morning with peroxide to prevent infection. Peroxide hurt very much, and the cows kicked hard enough to break a person's arm. We couldn't forget that. He also had to mend the neighbor's fence and pay him for the loss on his cane. To keep the cows from breaking down the fence again, he had to drive over to the northwest of us to buy ground-up thistle weed to feed them. "The man that runs the grinder is making money hand over fist," Daddy reported when he returned. "For sure what we spent dug a hole into our meager cash reserve."

But in the long run, we realized our losses weren't tragic. People were dying from dehydration and heat strokes. "Rain, more than anything, could save us," said Mother frequently.

I felt lucky that we had our wonderful well water in our

pasture for cooking and drinking, despite the fact that I had to carry it from there to the house.

And it appeared that we were famous for our outstanding well water. One day, Wanda May asked, "Could I come to your house to play so I can sample your famous well water?"

After I talked to Mother, I invited Wanda May to come the following Saturday. Her daddy brought her in the morning and said he wouldn't pick her up until after supper.

What a wonderful day! I even gave up my onion that day because I finally had a playmate over and didn't want my onion breath to spoil the fun. A few weeks before that, Mother had taken some egg money and bought me a set of jacks, and I felt proud and happy to have a friend come play jacks with me, write stories with me, and talk with me about books we both had read. And I was glad she wanted to help me carry water from the well.

~

Getting water from the well was such a hard job that I often wished our cistern water was fit to drink. In the days before we bought our truck, Daddy had paid a man to bring barrels of water from Westin to fill our cistern. "Having our own truck gives us a new lease on our lives. The truck is a necessity for many jobs," said Daddy, "and now we can haul our own supply of water, too. But I hate to tell you, Molly May, there's so much dust that's blown into the cistern that it has to be cleaned before we can add any more water."

An enormous amount of dirt from the dust storms certainly had sifted in through the cracks between the boards in the cistern's aboveground cover. The dirt had settled on the bottom and caused us to have to strain the water as the water level dropped. "And the problem is," Daddy continued, "we don't have a ladder that's long enough to reach the bottom, and I don't want to borrow one from the neighbors, if I can help it." To prove his point about the dirty cistern, he held the flashlight so Mother and I could see the mud.

Following our inspection, Daddy said, "Molly May, except for Tilley, you're the lightest in the family. I could lower you down to the bottom in a five-gallon bucket with a long rope tied on its handle." I shook my head from side to side in fear and took a step back. But he went on to say, "You could stand in the bucket and hang onto the rope."

So there I stood, shaking in my shoes, so to speak—the barefoot designated cistern cleaner.

Worried my clothes would be ruined, Mother rushed inside to create a cistern cleaner uniform for me. She took the oldest of her old housedresses and cut it shorter, but of course not so short that it wouldn't cover my bloomers.

"Stand as still as a statue in that bucket," Daddy said as he began to lower me into the darkness, "so you won't make the bucket sway and bump against the concrete walls of the cistern. Might cause you to lose your grip on the rope and knock you right out of that bucket."

I didn't need to be told more than once to stand still. I was scared stiff as a statue. The flashlight tied loosely around my waist rotated to and fro as the bucket swayed, making eerie movements of light on the cistern's murky bottom. Almost as scary as our dungeon cellar.

When I reached the bottom, I stepped out of the bucket and moved to one side. Daddy lowered a smaller bucket with a short-handle shovel in it. Each of the ten or so times I shoveled a bucketful of mud, Daddy pulled the bucket up and dumped its contents in a pile to be hauled away later by wheelbarrow to a nearby spot where a garden might flourish next season. That is, if we could give the garden enough water or if we finally would get some rain.

Each time Daddy moved away from the cistern to dump out the mud, Mother's head would pop over the edge and she'd chatter to me. I suspected her purpose was to take my mind off my misery, and to this day I can recall fragments like, "The garden could use the topsoil that's down there ... You're doing good work, Molly Girl ... As soon as you're done with this, we're going to get nice, clean water for this mighty clean cistern."

It was nice to hear that Daddy and Mother expected that I would get the cistern clean, but I couldn't help wishing Tilley would soon be old enough and bold enough to become the designated cistern cleaner. Of course, I was glad to have water in our cistern again. I was getting very tired of having to carry extra water from the well for the chickens, our baths, and many other cleanup chores.

When I finally had scooped up all the mud I could, Daddy sent down a whisk broom so I could whisk the rest of the mud into the shovel and then brush the mud from the shovel into the bucket. I did that again and again until the bottom of the cistern looked clean enough. But that wasn't the end of it. "Molly Girl, sweet hardworking girl," Mother called down, "we're sending down some rags and a clean bucket of water so you can mop the cistern clean."

"As if I could get the rough concrete clean in a million years," I mumbled to myself, regretting my attitude immediately. Luckily they couldn't hear me up above.

When I finally emerged from the cistern, my cleaning uniform was plastered with mud and so was I. Even my hair had caught splats of mud from the bottoms of the buckets when Daddy pulled them up. But before I could rush into the house to bathe, my folks said they needed to get rid of most of the mud that covered me. They poured dippers of well water all over my uniform and me—from my head to my toes. The air was stifling hot and dry, and I welcomed being splashed with the cool water.

When Mother finally told me I was clean enough to go into the house, I felt so good that I grabbed Daddy's dipper, filled it with water, and dashed some water on his chest. Mother instantly filled her dipper and doused him, too. I showered Mother, and she splashed me right in my face. But it all came to a sudden halt when Mother realized our folly and said, "Water, water, nowhere near and nary a drop to waste."

Daddy snorted and asked her where that had come from, and she admitted she might have read a line something like that once in one of her grandfather's old college books. Daddy turned away muttering something about fine-haired educated people. Mother's grandfather, a city man, was a college-educated minister turned politician and eventually an Arkansas state legislator. I felt uncomfortable that Daddy was cynical about him. I had seen him a few times in Arkansas, and I remembered how tall and dignified he was, even at eighty-something. But I reminded myself that Daddy had earned everything in his life the hard way, and he didn't understand or respect the fact that hard work was also involved in earning an education.

Mother packed a lunch for us while I finished getting ready. And we were soon on our way to get clean water for the cistern. My folks had said my work was done for the day, and I was thrilled to simply enjoy riding in our new truck while my baby brother slept in my arms.

During our ride home with the barrels of water, I tuned in to my folks' conversation. "Babe Ruth helped the Yankees win the World Series four times," Daddy said, "and the Yankees released him. It's a sad time for us fans of the Babe." I always liked it when Daddy talked about Babe Ruth, and so I felt a little bit sad about the Babe, too.

As we were nearing home, Daddy talked about Joe Louis and boxing. With baseball champion Babe Ruth no longer with the Yankees, I figured I would be hearing more about boxing matches in the future. I liked it when Daddy thought about something other than crop prices, drought, and the dust storms ruling our lives. At least that's how I felt right then, and I hoped when our clean cistern was filled with our fresh barrels of water, I would be better able to deal with the dry, hot weather. Maybe I'd be able to have washtub baths and shampoos twice a week instead of just once. Maybe the comb wouldn't be so full of dust when I combed my hair, or maybe my hair wouldn't have mud-stained sweat running out of it when the temperature soared.

~

Sometimes on a cooler morning during the long, hot summer, Mrs. Drecker, the kind neighbor who had helped take care of Mother the day of our tragic loss, stopped in for a visit. But one exceptionally hot day we were shocked to see her husband standing at our screen door, and he seemed either weak or frightened.

"Please, Mrs. Dowden, come with me to help take care of my wife," gasped Mr. Drecker, breathing like he'd just run a mile.

"Why, what's wrong?" asked Mother with concern, but without waiting for an answer, she continued, "I'll be glad to help. But I'll have to bring Molly May and the baby because my husband is in the field."

During the drive to the Dreckers' house we learned that the fragile-looking Mr. Drecker and his wife had been hoeing weeds in the small cotton field next to their house when he realized something wasn't right with his wife.

"She was staggering and talking like she was out of her head," said Mr. Drecker, his voice quivering.

"What did you do?" Mother asked, eyes wide open.

The poor man told us how he had tried to walk his wife, a big-boned woman, to their house, but before they could reach the house she had fallen to the ground crying and babbling nonsense. He couldn't lift her.

"Did you leave her outside?" Mother asked, trying not to sound alarmed.

"No. No, I didn't—not exactly anyway. I found two cardboard boxes in a closet and dumped out what was stored in them. Then I laid the boxes on their sides and put her head inside one and her feet inside the other. I stretched a narrow blanket from one box to the next to give her shade, and I squeezed some water into her mouth from a wet rag."

Mother told him he had done the right thing, and then she said, "By the way, do you have a wheelbarrow?"

Mr. Drecker told her he did, but with a puzzled look on his face. I didn't understand either.

~

Of course, scarcely anyone living in the country had an electric fan in those days. There was no electricity for most poor farmers! The Dreckers' kitchen was on the shady side of their house, and so it was the most comfortable room in their home. Still, it must have been a hundred degrees in the kitchen, where Tilley and I sat down and waited for Mother. Flies swarmed around Tilley, and I had to constantly fan them away with one hand while trying to keep him on my lap with the other. From the window I watched Mother and Mr. Drecker push the wheelbarrow across the dry, hard yard to the kitchen door. It was scary to see Mrs. Drecker curled up on her side in the wheelbarrow looking so helpless.

Her face was red as a ripe tomato, and it terrified me to see how wild-eyed she was. Mother, on the other hand, seemed calm. "The ice man delivered today, so do you have ice in your icebox?" she asked as soon as they had Mrs. Drecker inside the house.

When Mr. Drecker nodded yes, Mother told him that as soon as they could get his wife into a bed, he should bring some towels, old baby blankets, or whatever he might find that would be approximately the same size.

Mother promptly used the ice pick to chip off chunks of ice and put them in a large dishpan she had filled halfway with lukewarm water—naturally lukewarm, as it always was in the summer, unless it was fresh from a well or had been cooled with ice.

With Tilley in my arms, I followed Mother to the doorway where Mrs. Drecker lay on her bed, and I heard Mother say, "She's burning up, and her skin is red and dry. I think she might be having a heat stroke." Then she placed a cold, wet washcloth on Mrs. Drecker's forehead, wrung the cooled water from towels, and quickly placed them on Mrs. Drecker's body. She also wrapped pieces of ice in brown paper and tucked them under the poor lady's armpits and alongside her groin.

Then she tucked a cold washcloth inside Mr. Drecker's collar and draped a smaller cold towel over his head and said, "Here, fan her gently from head to foot with this folded newspaper. And give yourself a breeze with it once in a while, too."

A good day to shiver, I thought when Mother put a cold towel around my neck and another one around hers. Tilley seemed to squirm and whine from the heat. Mother picked up an old magazine from the dresser top, took Tilley from me, and walked toward the kitchen. I followed, and Mother sat down and nursed Tilley while fanning all three of us. The fanning kept the flies away as well.

By the time Daddy found Mother's note and came to get us in our truck, Mrs. Drecker was calmer, and she looked better. On the ride home I asked, "Mother, how did you know what to do to make Mrs. Drecker better?"

"Oh, I read about it in the Oklahoma City paper Mrs. Williams gave me the other day," she answered. "There was a list of things to do for someone who is overcome by the heat, and it was a great help today. I may have added a few things to the treatment for good measure, though."

Because I read only the comic strips, I hadn't known that kind of medical information was in the paper, but I had heard people were dying from the heat; and although it had been a scary day, I was very proud of Mother. I thought she might have saved Mrs. Drecker's life.

~

When Daddy dropped us off at the Dreckers' about a week later, we were carrying a tall layer cake. Mrs. Drecker's appearance was startling. She seemed to have shrunk in size, her eyes were sunken, and her face was a ghostly white. She also had fever blisters all around her lips, some scabbed over already, but bleeding a little when she talked. Clearly she was happy to see us, and she insisted, "Come on into the kitchen where it's cooler, and we'll have some lady talk."

Shooing away at least three dozen flies from the kitchen table, where they were feasting on corn bread crumbs, she said, "Sit down and have a piece of your cake with me."

I was accustomed to a clean table, and I wasn't used to having flies so thick in our house. Mother never permitted a fly to enjoy itself like that in her house for a moment before she used the fly swatter. When a lot of flies made it into our house, she flapped a dish towel in each hand and chased them toward the screen door, and then she commanded me at just the right moment to swing open the door. I quickly learned to move to the side while ducking down low and still managing to hold the door wide open so she could shoo the flies out through the open door.

I reminded myself that Mrs. Drecker had been sick and wasn't as young and peppy as Mother, and so her kitchen was overrun by flies. Then I decided to enjoy my slice of cake anyway. We'd so rarely had cake since we'd arrived in Oklahoma, and so I made up my mind that even if I might have to fight the flies for every bite, I would win that battle and eat my cake.

~

When Mrs. Drecker was well enough, she and Mother visited each other from time to time. But by the end of a summer of record heat, drought, dust storms, whirlwinds, and puny crops, rumors circulated that Mr. Drecker was driving around at night stealing turkeys from the well-off farmers. They said he stole turkeys instead of chickens because turkeys didn't make loud squawking noises when suddenly snatched from their roost.

Farmers talked of seeing him in the moonlight running humped over with a turkey in a sack on his back, and they'd put their guns away and say, "It's just old Edam Drecker."

He took only one turkey at a time from the well-to-do farmers around Thistleway and nearby communities, and when it was market time, he could be seen driving into town in his rickety truck hauling two or more cages of turkeys. Daddy said, "The funny part is, you could drive by the Drecker place any time of the day and never see a single turkey being raised there, but near market time there was a flock of grown ones roaming their yard."

"Well, Mr. Goody Two-Shoes Dowden, Mr. Drecker stole from the rich and gave to the poor—himself. Didn't he?" Mother said flirty-like, as she did sometimes to get Daddy to lighten up.

"In a way, he's a little bit like a person named Robin Hood in a story I read somewhere along the line," she quipped. Then she added, "Sometimes desperate times cause people to do desperate things." Daddy didn't say a word, and I was glad.

After that, she somberly pointed out that the Dreckers were as poor as church mice and that they were getting too old to work as hard as they used to at farming in the heat. She wondered how they would survive much longer at their age in such hard times, with their grown-up children living in another state, married with children and too poor to help them out.

"I read in the paper the other day that the government has passed a bill for Old Age Pensions. Well, actually, sounds like it will soon be called Social Security," Mother said, seeming to want to cast a better light on the subject of being old and poor, until she added, "but I guess no one will qualify for a while."

"Yeah, probably a good while," Daddy said. "Old man Drecker never had anything handed to him. Struggled all his life, I'm sure, trying to pull himself up by his bootstraps. Be mighty nice if he could have a pension. In bygone days, the old folks just moved into their married children's homes, but I wouldn't go for that."

"Social Security might keep us out of a bind like that when we're old," replied Mother, her voice sounding a bit sad.

Mother's sadness caused me to imagine myself as an older woman, too. I couldn't help hoping I'd have Social Security to help me live a more worry-free and healthier life. I certainly wanted to have a better late-in-life experience than my grandparents were having, or perhaps even my parents would have as they grew older.

Chapter Five

Although no other dust storm ever equaled the roller of April 1935, disabling dust storms were the norm the following year. To top that off, the summer of 1936 was again extremely hot and dry. Temperatures rose to 120 degrees almost daily.

People were dying of heat exhaustion, some just sitting in their homes—especially older folks. Since electricity was available only to those who could afford it, poor farmers had to endure the heat without any fans. And kerosene-fueled cookstoves could in the summer push an indoor thermometer to well over one hundred degrees. That kind of heat didn't confine itself to the kitchen, either.

"That cookstove heat feels as intense as a blacksmith's fire pit, and it sure knows how to turn corners to heat up the whole house," Mother said one day while escaping to the shade of the porch to fan herself for a few minutes with a folded newspaper. I thought how nice it would be if we could have an electric fan like some of the better-off farmers and people in town did.

~

Housewives had their ways of coping with the indoor temperatures that summer, but the farmers in the field had little escape from the heat. I could see that Daddy was at times both physically and mentally spent. Trying to follow the guidelines of the government's soil conservation program was just one more complication for him. You might say Daddy and a number of the farmers found it too much bother to follow the guidelines to the letter. The crops didn't improve, either, and many more farmers found they couldn't make enough from their crops to live on. They supplemented their income with part-time work on the WPA. Daddy, however, had part-time work for Mr. Curtis and continued to reject any work from the government.

"I draw the line as far as working on the WPA, but I agreed to rent my two strong plow horses to pull heavy road-construction equipment on nearby projects. What I mean is, when I'm not using them," Daddy said to Mother one morning at the breakfast table.

I was glad he had also agreed a while back to allow the Civilian Conservation Corps, known as the CCC, to plant a row of tall, slender trees across our backyard to deflect the winds. The trees also attracted scissor-tailed flycatchers, and I know I reaped some benefit from those birds. It was fun to watch them darting about with their long tails looking like they were poised to cut a piece of invisible cloth, and then landing on the trees for a rest and some bird chatter. How nice if the government could have stopped the dust storms, too, I thought to myself.

~

One morning at the breakfast table, my ears perked up when Daddy said, "I guess the government's highfalutin scientists are saying that the way farmers have been farming has caused the dust storms, and dust storms are causing problems up high in the sky, and that's why it doesn't rain."

"Yes, I remember Mrs. Bridges saying some of that when we lived in the shanty," Mother replied.

"Well, I reckon it won't hurt nothing if we try to go by the government's program. No telling what it'll be like in the next couple of years if we don't try something," Daddy acknowledged.

"I agree," Mother put in, "and while we're talking about the future, I might as well tell you I'm pregnant again."

Having just settled down to read in my bedroom, I wasn't supposed to hear that news. It was news I could be happy with, but I hoped our next baby wouldn't be as wiry and self-willed as Tilley. He had walked at nine months and now at one year was already talking in two-word sentences. He had to be watched every minute he was given the freedom to move about, and he howled for that freedom. I loved him dearly, but I hoped the next baby in our house would be a quiet little sister.

~

In spite of the unbearable heat that summer, it seemed Mother had found a way to keep Daddy from getting stressed and angry, at least sometimes. I labeled Mother's secret stress prevention, "tampering with the truth."

Once during a very hot spell, she had been busy most of the day with the tedious task of shelling peas and canning them for Mr. Curtis's wife on a "half for you and half for me" agreement. Mr. Curtis had driven all night to the east of us to purchase fresh peas for the canning.

I had been busy keeping Tilley out of mischief, when Daddy came in sweaty and dirty from the field.

"Did you have Molly May water the chickens three times today?" he asked Mother, his eyes looking skeptical and causing my heart to skip a beat. I had been reminded to water them only twice.

"H-m-m, maybe three times isn't enough today," Mother responded, not lifting her eyes from ladling the red beans from the pot to a serving bowl, and without even a guilty blink she glanced for a split second toward me and said, "Molly Girl, why don't you scoot on out and water them again while I finish getting supper on the table."

Daddy looked relieved after hearing Mother's guarded answer to his question, and he strode across the kitchen to the washbasin, where he scrubbed the dirt from his face, neck, hands, and arms in preparation for his supper.

I, on the other hand, rushed out the door to water the chickens, relieved that since he knew she was such a good Christian, he hadn't doubted her at all. I also reckoned Daddy was such a straight shooter that the idea of Mother messing with the truth had never even entered his head.

Finding the thirsty chickens with their beaks hanging open and panting like dogs made me feel guilty, and I quickly filled their trough with water a third time that day. At the same time I felt a little more grown-up for understanding that tampering with the truth in this case had served the good of everyone in my family.

~

Another autumn! Another season in the cotton field had come again, and school was closed for the usual two weeks. Daddy and

I would be doing most of the picking. The night before we were to begin, I tried hard to set my mind to it, and Daddy's talk at the supper table didn't help my attitude.

"I heard some farm machinery company is designing a better cotton-picking machine, one that won't damage the cotton plants. I doubt if that's true. Not that we could afford to buy one anyway. But I do know picking cotton is too hard a work for humans." Later as he rose from the table, he looked at me and said, "Tomorrow morning you and me are going to hit the cotton field just like we're made for the work."

The next morning it didn't seem much cooler than the killer summer had been, and I was already lonesome for school. But maybe I'd soon toughen up to the fieldwork, and time would pass quickly, I thought to myself as Daddy and I trudged toward the field.

"I wish the Gypsies would come again," I said to Daddy later when my sunbonnet caused my head to sweat so much that perspiration ran from my hairline into my eyes.

"Well, I don't think we have enough cotton this year for them to bother with," Daddy replied. "Look at how we're having to crawl on our knees most of the time to pick the bolls off these short plants." His mild attitude made me feel better.

But it didn't matter how scarce the bolls were on the plants. The distance we spent walking on our knees made our work even more grueling. Understandably, Daddy and I were plenty tired at the end of the day. "There's no rest for the wicked," Daddy sometimes said when he went right from the field to the milking. I, on the other hand, went inside to help Mother with supper, working with one hand while holding Tilley on my hip with the other. My long absence when I was in the field seemed hard for him. That filled me with a tender feeling, and I couldn't help worrying that he would miss me very much when I went back to school.

~

It seemed like months instead of two weeks before school resumed after cotton picking that fall, and I was happy there wouldn't be any more breaks for more cotton picking for a long, long time.

I missed last year's fifth-grade teacher. But I liked Miss Harkey, my sixth-grade teacher, because she tried to make our health habits sessions fun, and she treated us like we were older than we actually were. One example, which wasn't very much fun, however, was when she stressed that we should spread our clothes over chairs at night to air out so they would be fresher when we put them on the next morning. I didn't like being reminded that I didn't have enough clothes to change every day or two and that my mother might not wash them often enough. Of course I suspected—practically hoped—that some of my classmates felt as I did.

She moved on to talking about how important it was to do good daily washups between weekly washtub baths. Some students, especially the boys, couldn't help snickering. But Miss Harkey surprised us all when she said, "Jack, could you tell your classmates how hard it is to keep one's self clean living in all the dirt we're forced to endure?"

I held my breath for a second wondering what the would-be class clown would do with that and how Miss Harkey would react to his silliness. Jack should have known better, because he was a lot older than the rest of us. He had to repeat first and second grades due to so many days of missing school recovering from mumps and scarlet fever, and nearly dying from smallpox and other sicknesses. But even though he was older, he wanted to be as silly as a fourth-grader.

"My maw, she takes me by the scruff of my neck and tells me my ears are so full of dirt, potatoes could grow in them," Jack began. "Then it feels like she has a pitchfork in there when she digs in them with a washrag over her long, sharp finger. The creases in my neck are so full of dirt that it looks like my neck has stripes going around it, until Maw gets ahold of me, and man-o-man, can she scrub."

The boys laughed more than the girls.

"Yeah," Jack continued, encouraged by the boys' approval. "And when she's done, my neck feels raw as my you know what when it's rode on a skinny horse all day without a saddle."

Some of Jack's younger friends really cracked up over that one.

"All right, Jack," Miss Harkey intervened. "Thank you. But maybe next time you can tone it down so your friends' giggle boxes don't flip upside down like first-graders'."

Then Wanda May held up her hand for permission to share, and she said, "Once when I forgot to wash the underside of my forearms, my mother noticed white streaks where the water had run down through the dirt clear to my elbows. I guess the white streaks happened when I reached up for the towel. But I hadn't noticed the water running down my arms. Whew, my mother got mad."

I recalled that I had done the same thing once, and Mother scolded me about my poor job of washing up. After that, I noticed sometimes when other kids held up their arms in class that they had white streaks running from their wrists to their elbows, too.

Following Wanda May's story, Miss Harkey announced that class group pictures would be taken the next day, and she asked the students to think about ways they could prepare for the event. Again, the class really did a good job of sharing. One shy boy spoke up and suggested we could change our weekly bath and shampoo night to the night before pictures would be taken. That way, we'd look and feel better for the picture. A couple of the less well-groomed farm girls mentioned that since most of us had to use bar soap as shampoo, we could splurge with the water and have an additional rinse with vinegar in it to cut the dull look of soap scum in our hair. "Oh, yes," Miss Harkey chimed in. "Shiny hair really looks good in a picture."

And Jack spoke up with, "Yeah, even on boys."

Dental care was also a topic in our health habits sessions. I had plenty of instructions on that at home. Mother had taught me to brush my teeth morning and night with a horrible mixture of salt and soda. And every few months she would shine a flashlight in my mouth to see if I had any cavities. Mother was my only dentist while I was growing up, and a good one, too. I didn't get a cavity until I was twenty-five. Of course, I should also mention there was natural anti-cavity fluoride in most of the well water in southwest Oklahoma. Another godsend was the free Ipana toothpaste the school soon gave to its students.

Nonetheless, I was pretty sure that the toothpaste giveaway program at school would end before long, and every two weeks when the teacher gave us another small tube and a recording chart, I was thrilled, and I dutifully recorded my twice-daily brushings with Ipana. Getting the teacher's gold star at the top of my chart at the end of each two weeks was important to me. It was proof I could do something to better myself, which sort of made up for the fact that I couldn't do anything about the climate and crop prices. Another freebie was the bar of Lifebuoy soap we were given every two weeks. Once Miss Harkey greeted us with, "Oh, how clean all you Lifebuoy soap users smell this morning!" If she had said that to encourage us to keep using the soap, I think it worked!

Her talk of Lifebuoy soap made me think about the itch, as we called it—a contagious rash that itched like crazy! We never found out what caused the rash, only how to treat it. It had come around every winter for the last three years. With the exception of one winter, I always had only a few bumps between my fingers, and at night Mother stood nearby while I smeared a mixture of sulfur and lard on the rash, and then put cotton gloves on my hands for the night. The next morning she'd boil the gloves in water with shavings of her homemade lye soap. That night and morning routine lasted until all signs of the rash had disappeared. How relieved I felt to be rid of its embarrassing telltale signs on my hands.

But one time the rash spread over my entire body, and at night I had to wear long-handle underwear, socks, and gloves over all the smelly mixture—causing a stench that traveled throughout the house and into the classroom at school. But the strange thing was, most schoolchildren had the rash at some time during the winter, yet no one ever mentioned it, although you could smell the sulfur mixture on a number of them. At home, frankly, the odor was of far less concern than other matters, including having enough to eat. Especially meat.

~

It seemed the difficult times would never end. The topsoil was still being blown away to other regions of the country. Rainfall still wasn't sufficient. Of course when we ran out of jars of canned vegetables, we had skim milk, bread, and a spare amount of butter and eggs. Some meals were just corn bread and red beans.

Back in the summer, Mother had canned jars of a weed called lamb's quarter, which we saved for the winter months, and it didn't taste bad with vinegar and chopped raw onions sprinkled over it. For once we were happy that at least weeds could still grow without moist soil.

Daddy certainly tried to do his part when the cupboard became nearly bare. He'd take one of his rifles and head for the pasture, where he usually could shoot one rabbit before the whole pack would scatter in all directions, or hide behind tumbleweeds or mesquite bushes. He'd also check out the creek, and once in a while he would bring home a quail or Teal duck. I really enjoyed the taste of everything Daddy bagged, and Mother cooked all wild game to a tasty doneness. I must admit quail and Teal duck weren't very meaty, but we appreciated what we had, especially in the winter when the wild game didn't come out into the open as much as it did when the weather was warm. Since there wasn't enough money by then to buy hog feed, or enough grass to raise beef cattle, we no longer had pork or beef; and when all of the vegetables Mother had earned canning for Mrs. Curtis were gone, we often had only rice, red beans, and corn bread—sometimes only corn bread and milk.

~

Tramps from time to time ventured off the highway to ask for food; they were worse off than we were. Mother never turned one away without at least asking him to sit on the porch while she brought out a little something for him to eat. Even if it was only a piece of corn bread and a glass of buttermilk, the tramp's eyes glistened as he reached with thin hands for the snack. Sometimes a tramp would be so pitifully thin and dirty Mother would offer him a washbasin, cloth, and soap to sponge off while he waited on the porch until she made him flapjacks made with flour, salt, baking powder, water, one small egg, and as little lard as possible in the frying pan. She served them without butter and only a little syrup drizzled on top. I was sure the tramp understood that Mother did the best she could without taking from her family.

No matter what they were served, I could see from my vantage point inside the kitchen that they chowed down like starving dogs. More than once I saw tears of gratitude after they had actually licked the plate for any grease left over. They always stepped close to the screen door and called out their shaky-voiced thanks to Mother before leaving. It made us realize all the more how much better off we were than some, and we were grateful for that. Still, word seemed to spread among these unfortunate family-men-turned-tramps that Mother was a generous soul— and over the years she continued to feed a little something to the tramps who happened to stop by our home.

~

The Dreckers weren't as bad off as tramps, of course, but there wasn't any part-time work for poor old Edam Drecker. Mother would take them her usual two pieces of fresh corn bread and two servings of cooked red beans once in a while. But during the winter Mother was feeling under the weather, and she didn't get around to checking up on them. During that cold spell, the mailman became suspicious when the Dreckers' mailbox filled up, and he notified the county sheriff.

As the mailman had feared, the Dreckers were found dead in their home. The coroner's report said they had died from natural causes. At the funeral, we overheard their son shed more light on the "natural" cause of his parents' deaths. "The coroner said their lungs had granulomas in them that probably were caused by breathing in the dust, and there was other respiratory damage due to inhaled dust, too, which probably led to untreated infections. So it was the darn dust storms that killed them," asserted the son.

On the way home from the funeral, my folks talked somberly about the dust storms and the harm they did to folks' health, and how sad it was when old people had to die uncared for and alone.

Mother said, "This nasty Depression has forced grown children in a lot of families to scatter to all parts to find work, especially way out west to California."

I sometimes wondered if perhaps Mother was afraid that she, too, would be alone at the end. But in spite of my memories of such concerns, looking back now, I believe most of the children of the Depression were able to transcend the reality of the hard times—for the most part, anyway. Mainly, they just wanted to get on with the business of being a child. It wasn't so easy for me. I was worried about the present, and the death of the Dreckers made me wonder about my parents' future, too.

When word spread about the death of the Dreckers, new talk concerning the number of turkeys Mr. Drecker actually had stolen circulated. And before long, there were speculations that the turkey thief hadn't been old Edam Drecker, after all.

I thought, *That just shows that people should think twice about spreading nasty rumors.*

~

When Mother deemed us in desperate need for something sweet, she'd make stove-top cobbler. It was nothing but vinegar in sugar water with rubber-textured dumplings cooked in the mixture. Skimping on the lard made the dumplings chewy instead of tender. Skimp on this, skimp on that; that's just the way it was. But I convinced myself the dumplings weren't that bad with a dribble of whole milk on them.

On the rare times when we had potatoes, Mother stretched them for two meals: one meal of mashed potatoes and potato cakes for the other. Potato cakes looked like pancakes fried crisp and brown. They were filling, cheap to make, and very tasty. I wasn't a grown-up, but I could tell Mother always did the best she could under the circumstances. Of course, my insatiable appetite probably enhanced the sensitivity of my taste buds.

In fact, my ravenous need for food as a growing preteen would at times cause a gnawing in my stomach that got the best of me. On days when I wasn't in school, soon after I'd eaten, or for sure midway between meals, I would sometimes sneak a handful of uncooked oatmeal and go stand by the chicken coop to eat it. That way, if a grain or two escaped between my fingers, it would be gobbled up quickly by a chicken. Chickens were sometimes very hungry, too. I had often seen them snatch a large grasshopper right out of the air and swallow it whole. I could see the poor chicken's throat muscles working hard as it tried to gulp the grasshopper down—still alive and twitching. *Too bad chickens don't have teeth,* I sympathized silently.

On the other hand, I was glad to see grasshoppers eaten. I remembered one summer when they flew in swarms so thick they darkened the sky. They flew in by the thousands—maybe millions—and destroyed an entire field of our young cotton plants overnight. And Daddy cried. I hadn't seen Daddy bite down on his frustration in that way, and it scared me as much as when he swore.

~

As I grew older and wiser, I began to observe and respect even more sides of my mother. Aside from her sometimes kid-glove way of handling Daddy's temperament, Mother wasn't always the demure, guarded thinker. She was a bit of a risk taker, too, keen on just plain getting things done.

One example of her take-charge response to a crisis was the way she dealt with a stray dog, known then as an egg-sucking dog—later popularized in country-western lyrics.

"I've seen it sneaking away from our chicken coop, and I've gone right out and saw there were no untouched eggs in the nests," she told me.

"Well, how do you know it was a dog?" I pressed.

"Oh, the dog sticks its tooth or claw into each end of the egg," she explained, "and it siphons out the egg from one of the holes. And the dog doesn't hide the evidence—you know, the empty eggshells with the holes in them."

After several days of waiting and watching to spot the dog sneaking into the chicken coop, she suddenly was standing right in front of me while I was dust mopping the floor. She practically grabbed the dust mop from my hands while saying, "Stay indoors and watch after Tilley."

I whined, "Why? I'm doing my Saturday chores."

"The dog's back. Here, take Tilley," she answered while thrusting him into my arms despite my protests.

Then she took one of Daddy's guns from the rack above the kitchen door and ran outside. I knew she was a very good markswoman with a rifle, because I had watched her and Daddy target practice once in a while just for fun when we lived in Arkansas. But in this case I was nervous anyway.

I quickly pulled a kitchen chair to the window, took Tilley on my lap, and watched Mother chase after the dog while at the same time attempting to take aim at him with the gun. Finally when she came to the cow lot with the dog in the lead, she stopped, propped the gun on a fence post, and fired. That dog would never eat anyone's eggs again.

"Don't tell your daddy I did that. I'll tell him when the time seems right," she said firmly, yet sadly, when she came back into the kitchen. "And keep Tilley occupied while I go outside and bury that poor dog," she instructed as she placed the gun back into the rack. I knew she felt bad about having to destroy a dog. She liked dogs. But eggs were an extremely important source of food for us, as well as income.

Mother's take-charge attitude emerged again not long after the dog episode. I was in the sitting room one balmy afternoon keeping Tilley quiet on my lap, massaging his toes gently while I read my book. Then suddenly she was right at my ear and quietly saying, "There's a big snake under the kitchen cabinet."

I feared snakes more than anything, and I yipped, "In the kitchen? How did it get there?" Then, gaining some control, I whispered, "Oh, dear, and Daddy's not here!"

"I know. I know, and I should have nailed a piece of wood over the large mouse hole I discovered yesterday in the kitchen as soon as I found it."

"Where's the mouse hole, and where's the snake now?" I quizzed as softly as I could. Mother leaned closer to my ear to inform me the hole was behind one of the back legs of the cabinet, and the snake was under the cabinet way back in the corner.

Our frenzied whispering made Tilley fidgety, and I had to hold him tightly to keep him from tumbling off my lap. More calmly then, Mother looked at me, put her finger to her lips to signal a sh-h-h, and began her instructions. "Hand Tilley to me," she whispered. "Then go out the front door and get me the hoe leaning against the chicken coop. We'll wait right here while you run out and get it. Bring it in here through the front door. I'll sit in the middle of our bed here and hold onto Tilley."

As soon as I returned, I handed Mother the hoe, took Tilley from her, and then sat in the center of Mother and Daddy's high bed and held Tilley firmly in my arms. I tried another method I used sometimes when I needed to keep him out of trouble. I gently massaged the palms of his hands and his fingers, and he didn't squirm or make a sound. Through the open door to the kitchen I could see Mother trying to put the hoe between the snake and the wall so she could drag it to the kitchen door and push it outside. At least that's what I assumed.

I could see it was awkward for Mother because our cabinet stood on legs and was only about a foot or so off the floor. The cabinet sat kitty-corner in the room, and in that corner the snake coiled and struck repeatedly at the hoe. No doubt about it, the snake was a fighter, and its venom spurted on the hoe with every strike. Finally Mother took a different approach. She held the broom in her other hand and used it to divert the snake's attention. As soon as the snake became aware of the broom, it tried to strike it, and the pioneer woman used that distraction to strike the fatal blow with the hoe right where the snake's neck would be, if it had a neck. Fortunately, Daddy kept our hoes very sharp.

When we were sure the headless snake was totally dead, we took a close-up look at it. We had heard of folks occasionally finding a rattlesnake in their houses in those days, but we knew rattlesnakes had rattlers on their tails. This one didn't. When Daddy got home, he took a look and then went to ask Mr. Williams to call Mr. Curtis and set a time for the two of them to come see the snake and tell us what kind of snake it was. They arrived within an hour, but not before Daddy had carried the very dead snake to the backyard, cleaned up the snake venom and blood, and nailed a board over the large mouse hole.

"It's a cottonmouth water moccasin," Mr. Williams said immediately.

"One of the deadliest snakes there is," Mr. Curtis added, verifying Mr. Williams's conclusion completely.

After that, Mr. Curtis told us that a little while back there had been a write-up in the Thistleway newspaper about two young boys shooting a six-foot-long cottonmouth water moccasin about three miles upstream from our section of the same creek. "Well, it's unusual to see that particular breed of snake around these parts," interjected Mr. Williams. Then he looked directly at Daddy and Mother and added, "And when the boys discovered it, it had strayed a ways from the creek, too."

~

When the early spring dust storms reentered our lives, cleaning up the dust, taking care of Tilley, and schoolwork dominated my thoughts. So I hadn't paid attention to how much Mother's stomach had grown during the last several months. But then on April 14, two years after Tilley's birth, Aaron, my second brother to be born on that date, arrived while I was in school. There was no dust storm on Aaron's arrival date though! No fuss, no bother would have been a good way to describe Aaron's birth, and him.

But all too soon, he would have to share my lap with a baby sister, Virginia Sue, and Tilley would become too rambunctious to sit on anyone's lap, except mine once in a while.

~

After our years of practice, we Dust Bowl dwellers had learned what we needed to do to survive the extreme weather conditions, coupled with the severe nationwide economic depression. And although it all was a very large package of challenges, we still didn't feel that any other single storm was as catastrophic as Black Sunday. So we took what we got and pretty much failed to store in our memories the details of the less severe storms and the challenges they presented. There was, however, one time when I experienced a different kind of weather event accompanied by a memorable concurrent event. That day jelled in my mind.

It was late February 1938, and I was in the seventh grade. I had been excited since back in the fall. Seventh grade was unofficially called junior high, and I was eligible to play basketball. I enjoyed playing very much, but weak ankles were my physical handicap, which by winter had caused me to miss some practices and two games. Night games out of town were my favorite because after the bus brought us back from the game, I was permitted to stay overnight at Wanda May's house.

On the day of the final out-of-town game of the season, Wanda May's brother gave me a note from her informing me she was very sorry but she was sick and I couldn't stay overnight.

That news meant I had to tell the coach I couldn't play in that night's game.

When I boarded the school bus for home at four o'clock, I left behind my regrets about missing the final game. But the bus engine was ailing, and we had to wait until a mechanic could finish fixing it; by the time the bus driver headed toward his route, it was late and the sky was looking very dusty.

As soon as I exited the bus at my corner by the gas station, I took off in a trot. The dust was getting thicker and mixed with snow. It was a snuster, or a snirt storm, as I liked to call it. Recalling that my teacher had spoken once about King Boreas of the north wind, I thought he must be pleased with this snirt stunt!

But regardless of my attempt to make light of the situation, I was worried and I switched from trotting to running. Soon my right foot landed on a small rock in the road, and my ankle flipped. Instant pain! Off balance and veering sideways, my ankle couldn't bear my weight, and I fell to the ground. When I stood up and tried to put my weight on my ankle, the pain was unbearable.

I crawled to a place where I'd not be hit by a passing car but could still be seen by the side of the road. I thought my treasured red wool coat, which my folks had scrimped to buy in a sale catalog for $1.59, would help to make me visible, too. The coat was three sizes too big for me so I could grow into it, and that turned out to be a good thing. I unbuttoned it just enough to slip my arms out of the sleeves. Then, lying facedown next to the road, I wiggled into my tubelike coat-turned-blanket until my head was inside and I didn't have to breathe in the dust. But I was exposed to the cold from my calves to my feet.

Although I kept very still so my coat would stay snugly in place, my mind clicked. *Thank goodness it's too cold for snakes and spiders to be around. My folks are thinking that I'm playing basketball and then staying overnight with Wanda May, and Daddy won't come looking for me. I might lie beside this road and freeze to death before anyone comes along.*

Then I thought I heard Mother's voice say, "Pray." I did pray, and after that I fell asleep for a while. When I woke up, I could feel a strange but wonderful warmth across my legs and feet. I remained still, fearing the warmth was not real, that my mind was playing a trick on me. More time passed, and I heard a car's engine in the distance, and at the same time I heard a dog's soft whine. Now I was sure my imagination was running wild. But when the car seemed quite near, I felt the weight of something lift from my feet and legs, and right away there was loud barking. Quickly I peeked from beneath my coat cover and saw Hattie, Mr. and Mrs. Williams's dog, standing near me, her light-colored fur illuminated by the car's lights.

I noticed when my rescuer helped me into his car that he was a man of about thirty and smelled like an empty whiskey bottle I once found on the roadside. But I immediately convinced myself my imagination was outdoing itself when he said he had stopped for supper and a visit with his mother after his work on the WPA. He was on his way home, which was a couple of miles on the other side of the Dreckers' old farm. As the nice man drove me toward my home, he said, "Considering the bus was late in dropping you off, you were probably in the cold for only about two hours." *Only about two hours*, I thought to myself. Even with the warmth of Hattie draped across my exposed legs and feet, my teeth were still chattering. But I responded, "Thank you, sir, for finding me. My parents will be grateful that you rescued me."

Later, Mr. Williams maintained that Hattie probably had picked up the scent of my fear from their place, which wasn't far from where I lay. But we never knew for sure if Hattie had picked up the scent and had come to my aid or if she had discovered me when she was returning from one of her stops by our house, where she anticipated receiving her usual pats and strokes.

After Mother and Daddy heard my story, Daddy said, "I'm really awful glad you're all right, but I don't understand why so many dangerous things happen so often to you, the careful one."

Mother, my eternal teacher, smiled wearily and said, "So you can figure that your prayer, your treasured red coat, and a dog saved your life tonight."

~

The summer after my very scary experience stranded outdoors during the snirt storm offered little difference from the scorching summer before. Again, we made sure we had plenty of well water on hand to keep ourselves hydrated, and we tried to stay indoors or in the shade as much as possible. Quiet time helped. But kids will be kids.

At times my younger brothers' playful scuffling and my baby sister's crying or jabbering made our house seem a little rowdy. Daddy usually would give the boys his disapproving look, verbal scolding, or a swat or two on their bottoms. Other times, when Daddy was in a good mood, he would act silly and he'd say, "All it takes to make me happy is three little kids to call me Pappy. One in the corner, one in the cradle, one in the trash bucket up to his navel." Other times, he'd say, "We get a new baby more often than we get rain." Humor was one of Daddy's good ways of managing stress, and I remember those times fondly.

~

By the time I was in eighth grade, it seemed like we were getting a little more rain, and instead of so many dust storms that began in late winter, we were blessed with snusters. And when the weather warmed up, we learned that in some nearby areas there were farmers who benefited from the government's push for irrigation technology that made use of their plentiful underground water—artesian wells, they called them. All that resulted in better crops for those farmers and made us feel like we might be turning the corner for a better life, too. In reality crop prices remained low, and the Depression lingered.

~

I must say Daddy didn't just wait for better times to happen. He took a few hours about once a month to attend cattle auctions. He would buy one or two yearlings to fatten up for a while in our slowly recovering pasture, and then he would take them back to an auction a short time later to sell for a profit. He also increased his milk-cow herd, and the cream separator motor in the kitchen whirred every morning and night. I had foreseen that picture from the start. I knew I would be the one turning the crank endlessly to make the motor whirl. But it really wasn't so bad. Without losing my rhythm, I could let my thoughts wander while I vigorously turned the crank.

We and other farmers were selling more cream and eggs than ever. A couple of the formerly less well-dressed farm girls were getting beauty-shop perms and wearing store-bought dresses of noticeably better fabric than flour sack material. I didn't dress any better or have a perm. Not by choice, however. Neither did most of the other farm girls, I suspected.

At least Daddy had finally bought a ladder and repaired the crack in our cistern, and it would hold all the rainwater that would drain to it via the gutters on the house. Eventually, with more rain, we would have enough water in our cistern to keep our clothes and bodies clean.

Perhaps best of all, the kids in school were no longer coughing from breathing in dust as much as they had before, and the odor of the mustard plaster for our lung congestion eventually became nothing but skimpy notes in my old journal. The telltale stench of the sulfur and lard mixture used for the itch was no longer detectable, either.

Was that because we had more water and better hygiene? Perhaps. We'd never know for sure why the rash epidemic disappeared. In any case, how nice it must have been for the teachers to no longer have to smell the stench or to witness their students scratching themselves.

~

"Rain and better crops could mean the Dowden kids won't have to wear ragged shoes that are too small, isn't that right?" I asked Mother one night when rain was dripping into the buckets we had placed under the leaks in our ceilings.

"I think it won't be long before you, my sweet Molly Girl, will have better shoes and dresses," she replied. "And your daddy and I feel four children make enough young Dowdens in this house."

I could live with that, I thought. Being the big sister and part-time mom to Tilley, Aaron, and my sweet little pal, Virginia Sue, made it seem like a houseful to me—and in truth, a lot of work.

~

The summer between my eighth- and ninth-grade years started off well. I managed to spend some alone time with my summer reading. Two Pearl Buck novels my eighth-grade English teacher had loaned to me were among the several borrowed books on my shelf, and I could hardly wait to read those about Pearl Buck's China. I was grateful that my teacher wanted me to read many different kinds of books.

Sometimes I would close my eyes to rest between chapters and think about how good it was not to be so shy or insecure anymore. I had been lucky to have two good eighth-grade women teachers who were young, smart, well-dressed, and caring role models.

In fact, one of them, Miss Carson, my English teacher, complimented me on my appearance or my writing skills every time she could. She fed my self-confidence even more when she gave me such compliments in front of the other teachers. But it was especially uplifting when she bestowed those compliments within hearing distance of the popular girls who were always voted class president or secretary or Miss Junior High. None of that motivated me to become outgoing like they were. But at least I pumped up my self-esteem knowing I was a better student, and I pictured myself someday as a teacher. My fantasy of me as a model in a catalog wearing pretty clothes would sometimes pop into my head, too. What a lasting impression my days of perusing the old Sears catalog had made on me! *How much longer will I have to tell myself not to be sidetracked by such an unrealistic ambition,* I wondered.

For the most part, I was learning how to handle my self-doubts back then, and I was happy with my own coterie of friends. But at home that summer after my eighth-grade year, there was one incident when I didn't handle my attitude so well toward Daddy.

It was a hot morning, and Mother and I were sitting in the shade of our house shucking two tubs of corn Mr. Curtis had driven all night to purchase fresh from a farmer near Oklahoma City. Because his wife was having health problems again, Mother had agreed to can all of the corn for one-half of the yield. So we were pressed for time and working fast and hard when suddenly Daddy came around the corner of the house carrying two buckets of milk from the barn.

"I want you both to keep an eye on the cows today. They're on the north side of the pasture where I won't be able to see them from where I'll be working," he announced before we quite realized he was there.

"I know, Tillman," acknowledged Mother, picking up another ear of corn. "There's not much grass there, and they might break down Mr. Gwen's fence." But her attempt to let him know that she and he were on the same page didn't seem to soothe him.

"So watch them!" he continued, his eyes widening. "They might break through the fence and hurt themselves on the barbed wire and gorge themselves on his cane like they did the last time." Then he looked at me and added, "You hear? One cow bloated up from eating too much cane and died, remember?"

I heard him, but I didn't answer right away. I was thinking about how hot it was already and how it was bound to get hotter before my day's work would be done. The house would be like an oven all day while we cut the corn from the cob and put it into the jars. Then we would process the jars of corn about a half dozen at a time for about an hour in a boiling, steaming cooker. Hour after hour, one after another, there would be a boiling, steaming cooker filled with jars of corn on the stove.

Dreading all that, I was already walking on a thin string. I resented having to work so hard in the extreme heat while helping to entertain my siblings so they would stay in the shade. Now it was "watch the cows." So I sassed him.

He set the buckets on the ground and took a step toward me, and I feared he would twirl me around and swat my behind, but he only pointed at me and yelled, "Watch your mouth, and just do your part for this family."

Do my part, I fumed to myself. I had tiptoed around my daddy all my life and had suffered very little of his wrath directly, but in that moment of teen rebellion, I had asserted my feelings. And instead of feeling I had come of age, it all amounted to Daddy's words seeming like a slap to my face. My daughterly feelings for him were severely bruised, to say the least.

That night at the supper table remorse was written all over his face, and he said, "Sister," which he called me only when he was feeling kind toward me, "I have to go to town in the morning. Would you like me to buy you the pair of yellow ankle socks I heard you say you wanted to go with your Sunday dress?"

My bitterness melted like a spoon of cold butter in a warm pan, and I thought for a few seconds before looking directly at him. Then I answered, "Thank you anyway, but I've decided I don't need the yellow ankle socks. My beige socks will be fine with that dress."

~

Around the time I was transitioning from grade school to high school, farming methods were moving toward mechanization, even for the small-scale farmers. Daddy and other farmers took advantage of the government-backed loans and bought tractors and a few other pieces of necessary farm equipment.

Autumn cotton-picking times had almost ceased in our vicinity because more of the farmers, including Daddy, had already given up raising labor-intensive cotton in exchange for growing corn, cane, maize, oats, and mostly winter wheat. One reason for switching to winter wheat was because it would be well rooted by the time dust storms would begin in late winter, and that helped greatly to keep the soil from blowing away. The occasional rains helped significantly as well.

I enjoyed helping Mother with the cooking for Mr. Curtis's harvest crew when they came to cut our grain, and I was ecstatic we no longer had cotton picking to look forward to.

But in the big world a dark cloud loomed. I was aware of it because Mother listened daily to the radio while she did her housework. At the supper table, I'd hear her telling Daddy about America's uneasiness concerning the German dictator, Adolf Hitler. I might have listened more closely had I known then that my country would soon be in a war that would change my life profoundly and the world forever.

~

Like other families, we had become so frugal during the worst of times that we'd squeeze a dime until it hollered, as Daddy liked to say.

But times were improving ever so slowly, and we did dress a little better, and the whole family would occasionally go to town for a joyful event. There were rodeos and carnivals, and a traveling repertoire theater performed in a tent for three nights in a row every season. The rodeos were free, and the tent plays cost a mere pittance.

Daddy and Mother were never more carefree than when we attended the tent theater. In addition to shelling out for the tickets, they bought a large bag of popcorn for the family to share during the performance.

For the rodeo, Tilley and I each were given a nickel to spend on cotton candy, which we had to share with our younger brother and sister.

At the carnival, sometimes the operator of the Ferris wheel would allow one of my younger siblings to ride on my lap free of charge.

All that fun for just a few cents! It didn't take big things, then, to make us happy. And clearly, my family benefited from the exhilaration of being a part of community life. I actually felt upbeat just being in Thistleway. I wasn't inflating my perceptions of such feelings, either. After all, my teachers had mentioned that it was a tiny town with a vibrant history and a progressive outlook. I surely had a sense of that, and when all of the traveling entertainments, one by one, had gone on to a warmer climate, I lived for an overnight at Wanda May's house.

Since my overnight visits at her house were usually prearranged when there was a school event such as a girls' softball or basketball game, a spontaneous invitation to stay overnight was even more exciting.

"Oh, that would be so swell," I would respond to Wanda May's unexpected invitation to stay overnight with her. "But I stayed overnight only a little while ago, and I don't think Daddy will let me again so soon," I answered in exaggerated disappointment, hungry for more town life. Just walking one block from her house to the main street to buy a Tootsie Roll for a penny, when I had a penny to spend, made me feel carefree.

I liked to be at Wanda May's for another reason. She and her twin brother, Jeremy, were the youngest in the family, and there weren't little siblings running around tugging on my skirt. It was like a little vacation from my seemingly never-ending chores and looking after my younger siblings. After a little time away, though, I was always glad to return home to my brothers and my sister.

~

By September 1939, the opinion of news-savvy adults had been passed on to young people, and statements like this were heard: Hitler has already tromped into Austria and Czechoslovakia. Now he's invaded Poland, and who knows how many other countries will be next. And he openly said he wants to get rid of all Jews; plus his agenda is America after he conquers Europe and Britain.

In spite of the unease about the turmoil overseas, my high school life as a freshman and sophomore became more and more filled with activities. I played varsity softball and basketball. I was especially excited about basketball, and being tall, I was a natural when both of my ankles were healthy. One of Oklahoma's progressive moves had been its girls' basketball program. Every school had one, and the girls' games were a big event in every community—right up there in importance with the boys' games. Knowing teenage girls were important enough to warrant this attention made us girls feel good.

~

In the fall of 1941, when I was a junior, dislike of Germans had become so intense that people were happy Joe Louis, a black man, was still going strong as the world champion boxer instead of Max Schmeling, a German by birth.

Fear mixed with an air of exhilaration regarding America's getting into the European fray could be sensed among the older teens, especially the boys. Then on Sunday, December 7, 1941, Pearl Harbor was brutally attacked. By December 8, these fragments from President Roosevelt's radio message reverberated in our minds: "a date which will live in infamy ... our interests are in grave danger ... we will gain the inevitable triumph. So help us God."

The president's proclamations plucked our strings even more—and intensified our feeling, *we can do.*

"The day I graduate I'm joining the army, or I'm going to California to work in a defense plant," announced Jack, the former would-be class comedian, now filled with patriotic resolve. Other boys picked up on it.

Girls even talked of leaving right after graduation to work in a defense plant in California. But I was sure Daddy wouldn't allow me to go to California, and so I didn't talk about it to anyone, except to Wanda May and Mother. They both said that perhaps some kind of miracle would happen after I graduated, and I would go to either California or somewhere even better. I dared to hope for better. After all, there were discernible signs of better economic times in our country—and in our area.

~

As the war fronts expanded, our history teacher increased his references to the war. One day he said, "Most of you have survived the severe poverty and deplorable southwest climate of the 1930s, and underneath you are well grounded."

Unbeknownst to the teacher or us, we were indeed destined to be among the millions of Americans who would be lauded in Tom Brokaw's book *The Greatest Generation.* I must admit I'm proud of that.

So in the face of the talk about the draft, most of the eleventh- and twelfth-grade boys wore the mantra "I'm ready to fight." But they wanted the assurance that when they returned as men from the war, there would be a man's life waiting for them, a wife or a sweetheart. The words of the then-popular song, "Don't sit under the apple tree with anyone else but me till I come marching home," became the would-be soldiers' courting theme. It was as if they were already on the troop train, and their girlfriends, who had promised to be the faithful wife or sweetheart, were standing on the train platform waving good-bye.

I was not one of those girls; I didn't have a boyfriend. But in my own way I resonated with the patriotic ambiance of it all.

~

At home my life seemed somewhat easier. My two youngest siblings appeared to be less dependent on me. Even so, I was glad Mother and Daddy had decided four Dowden offspring would be enough. But in the spring of my junior year, my youngest brother, Wilson, was born. I couldn't wait to teach him the ABC song and many other skills at an early age, as I had done with the others. Before long, we all thought he was a quick study. Mother put in her two cents' worth once when she said, "Well, of course he's smart. I nursed all my babies until they were old enough to slide off my lap, turn around, and say 'thank you.'" That was true, but we all giggled anyway.

Mother was often ahead of the times in her theories, and she could be either commanding, demur, or wry. I appreciated all sides of her, most of the time.

I had turned sixteen the month before my senior year, and Mother teasingly said that because I was now sweet sixteen and never been kissed, I could go out with boys for special school events. That old saying made me recoil internally. I don't mean to say I didn't appreciate the humor, but for my own mother to tease me about getting myself kissed, whether I was ready or not, went against the grain a little, in spite of the fact that I really liked for boys to notice me—in respectful ways. But so far, I hadn't had the yen to be kissed by any boy other than Frederick or Jeremy. Truthfully, *that* had only been hope for a kiss on the cheek, like I'd seen Daddy sometimes plant on Mother's cheek.

~

In the midst of the rampant talk of war, a senior named Garrett asked me to be his date for the Future Farmers of America spring party in the home of the agriculture teacher, and I accepted. But I didn't accept because I wanted him to kiss me. Goodness, no! It was bad enough that he was shorter than I was—girls simply weren't supposed to be taller than their dates in those days. I measured five foot eight inches, and he was only about five foot six, but muscular. I imagined the two of us entering the party side by side, and I would look as though I were his older sister. Unfortunately, it took me a while to realize society had fostered the idea that petite was neat, not tall; and it took me even longer to admit that my own mother had unwittingly sent me the same message. In truth, she often verbally called attention to the appealing physical attributes of only the shorter girls or women and seemed not to appreciate my size—or hers.

Although my date with Garrett wouldn't be a dream social night out, a date was a date. I needed to get some practice in social talk one-to-one outside of school before I was out of high school. So I let up on my imagined double date with some cute, tall boy and Wanda May and her boyfriend from another school. That date would have been the four of us going to a movie in Westin and having an ice cream cone afterward. But I knew I should hold back on such extravagant thoughts, because money still wasn't the least bit plentiful in most families. And part-time jobs for high school boys were practically nonexistent at that time in the Thistleway area.

~

The Future Farmers of America party was low-key, and that was fine. But the ride back to my house that balmy spring night turned into a nightmare.

When we were about halfway between the main road and my house, Garrett suddenly pulled the car toward the shoulder of the narrow dirt road. "What's wrong?" I asked, sure there was car trouble and worried we'd have to walk the rest of the way and wake Daddy to give Garrett a hand. Daddy didn't like to have his sleep disturbed.

"Nothing's wrong," Garrett finally answered in a strangely husky voice as he turned off the engine.

Then without another word, he sprang on me and clamped his wet mouth on mine with such force that my head was pinned against the back of the seat. Turning my head side to side in protest caused his teeth to hurt my mouth, but it didn't deter him. I managed to get my arms between us, but I couldn't push him away. I yanked his hair and twisted his ears, and I thought I might have scratched his neck and jaw, but everything I did to him was barely more effective than a pestering gnat. Finally he stopped kissing me—or whatever he thought he was doing. Then he began groping at my blouse buttons. I shoved away his hands while repeatedly crying out, "Stop it!" Finally he shifted his hand to my knee, and I became a person not like me, just as I had the day I hit Vera Lou in the face.

"What is the matter with you?" I shouted, before slamming myself forward and biting his arm, hard. That stopped him. Then while he momentarily cradled his arm in his other hand, I took advantage of the moment and braided my long, thin legs. At the same time I tried to distract him with my rapid-fire hits to his bicep and shoulder. I felt like my arms were the arms of someone else, not me. Garrett brought me back to my senses, however, when he said, "Stop, Molly. You're hurting me. Your arms are whirling like windmill blades on a windy day!"

Garrett moved away from me then, but I wasn't certain the ordeal was over. I reached for the car door handle, opened the door, shook my head, and quietly said, "Garrett, I like you, but have you gone daffy?"

He didn't say anything, but as both my feet touched the ground, I heard, "Molly, wait." Then a pause before he said, "Cripes, Molly, this is my first time out with a girl, and maybe I don't know how to act. And this here war has got me feeling afraid I'll be killed before I have a chance to know what it's like to—well, you know."

"Oh, Garrett," I replied. "I don't understand why you picked me for that. I don't ever act one bit flirty or anything."

"Well, you always walk around school with your back as straight as a stick, and your breasts are—well, noticeable."

"What?!" I exclaimed. "Now, that takes the cake. You're saying all of this is my fault!"

"No. No, I'm not," he responded, while sliding over the seat, coming through the still-open door and then jumping onto the ground quite near me—too close for comfort. "Listen, what I said didn't come out right," he continued as he took a quick step back, seeming to think I might strike him again. "I'm sorry about that and this whole thing. I'll take you the rest of the way home in a minute. But first—uh-h-h, look, Molly, I won't tell anyone about this if you won't."

"Don't worry!" I spat over my shoulder as I jumped away from the car and turned my back to him, determined to get home on my own. But instead of leaving instantly, I turned around and added, "If I tell one single person about this, my daddy will surely find out, and he will shoot you like he would a jackrabbit. And I don't want my daddy to go to prison."

I heard Garrett suck in his breath before his second plea for my promise not to tell, no matter what.

I promised, pleased my exaggeration of Daddy's reaction had seemed so effective. Then I said, "And I'll tell you one more thing—I'm not going to walk around school or anywhere else bent over like a monkey with my arms dangling down in front of me so my breasts won't be noticeable."

Without a word more, I marched down the dirt road to the safety of my home. With that, I ended my first and last date with a local boy.

At school on Monday morning, Garrett and I were walking in the same hallway to our classes, but as usual, not together. I heard him say to the boy walking next to him that his facial scrapes happened when he fell from a tractor and landed on the trailer hitch. I wondered how anyone could believe he wouldn't have been bruised, too. But mercifully, the outcome of the boys' Friday baseball game was uppermost in most students' minds. And so Garrett's story about falling off the tractor didn't give anyone pause for thought.

For the first few days after my awful first date, I tried not to think about what had happened. Without realizing then that most women and teen girls in those days would have felt as I did from such an experience, I feared it would reflect badly on me if anyone found out. Fortunately, I didn't carry that burden very long before I accepted in my heart Garrett's brief outburst regarding how the war had influenced his behavior that spring night.

So I kept our secret—Garrett's and now mine—even from Mother and Wanda May, and I've always been glad I did. A few years later I learned that Garrett had been killed fighting for his country in the Battle of the Bulge and was posthumously awarded the Medal of Honor.

Chapter Six

It was the day after my graduation, and Tilley and I were returning from the well in the late afternoon with our buckets of water when I noticed a sleek two-door car parked in our yard. Wondering who it might belong to, I left Tilley behind and rushed ahead to the house. With each step I felt my spirits rise a little more, hope inexplicably warming my heart.

"And this has to be Molly May," said the attractive, well-dressed woman when I stepped into the kitchen.

"Just Molly," I said, instantly regretting it. I had sounded curt unintentionally.

I recognized her. With her last Christmas card she had sent a picture of herself standing by her car. At the sight of her in person, I felt myself about to slip back to my shy phase. But then I caught myself.

"I remember you—you're Maribelle," I said, scanning her hat, dress, shoes—probably not too subtle in doing so.

Then I told Maribelle how much I had appreciated all the times she'd sent me a pair of knee-high socks, especially the pair she sent me when I was around ten years old. I reminded her that they had wide green and yellow horizontal stripes. And to let her know how much those socks had meant to me, I admitted that I had slit the ends of the toes when they became too small for me and had worn them for about two years longer.

"Well, sounds like you're thrifty like your mother," Maribelle said with a nice smile.

"I was just telling your mother I was sorry to barge in without letting you all know, but it was Saturday and I was off work for two days, and I had a sudden urge to just get in the car and drive on out to see you, and you don't have a phone."

"We haven't felt a great need for a phone," Mother cut in, "but we might get one if many more people barge in on us." Then she laughed, and Maribelle did, too.

Mother apologized for not having a bed for her to spend the night, unless she wouldn't mind sleeping in a bed with me and Virginia Sue. "In the same room where the other bed will be filled with two boys and toddler Wilson," Mother said. Much to my surprise, Maribelle said that would be all right!

At the supper table, Maribelle asked me what kind of work I would be doing now that I had graduated, and I told her I was trying to get a job at the new little hamburger place in Thistleway.

"But will you make enough to pay your room and board?" Maribelle asked with concern.

"My friend Wanda May's brother Jeremy has volunteered for the army, so I can stay at their house. It won't cost me very much."

Maribelle smiled faintly at me and nodded as though she understood. Then she turned her attention to my family and convinced all of them to sit on the porch to cool off while she and I did the dishes.

As soon as we were alone, Maribelle surprised me by asking if I had a boyfriend. I no doubt blushed. Then I told her that my folks wouldn't allow me to go out with boys before I was sixteen, and by the time I was sixteen the popular girls and the nicest boys were already couples. I also told her I had been absolutely crazy about Wanda May's twin brother, Jeremy, but he never paid any attention to me. Maribelle didn't say anything.

"Why did you ask?" I finally asked her.

"Well, I just wanted to know if you have a good reason for staying around Thistleway. You're a very pretty girl, and you have excellent posture and a good slim figure like a fashion model. Let me ask you if working in a hamburger place is what you would like to do with your life?"

"What I'd like to do is work in a defense plant," I answered. "But the defense plants are in California, and Daddy would never let me live in California. I *am* younger than my classmates, you know." Maribelle nodded again and then changed the subject.

"I haven't even told your Daddy yet, but my brother worked in town the first winter after you and your folks left Arkansas, and he was offered a full-time job. He decided that he didn't want to be a farmer."

I couldn't begin to imagine what I'd hear next.

"So I rented the farmland to a neighbor all those years, until I had a very good offer right after last Christmas from a company that wanted to make a chicken farm out of it."

She then told me she had recently moved to Oklahoma City to work in a defense plant that made airplanes for the military.

"I never heard anyone at school mention there was a defense plant in Oklahoma City," I said, amazed.

"I know," she said. "Everyone thinks the defense plants are all in California. And I'm saving the best for last."

Again, I couldn't imagine what I'd hear next, and if I could have imagined it, I would have sat down in case I might faint like

I almost did once before. But I managed to ask what she meant, recalling she had suggested the *best* was still coming.

"Well, I talked to your mother about this soon after I got here, because she mentioned your desire to work at a defense plant. Here it is: would you like to come back with me to Oklahoma City?"

Her invitation was both a shock and a dream come true.

"Oh, Maribelle, this is a miracle," I said, trying not to come unglued from emotion. Maribelle made mother-hen sounds while patting my shoulder. "Right now," I continued, my emotions still in check, "I want more than anything to work for my country. My dream of becoming a teacher or a model can be put on hold while I do that. It would give me a chance to save enough money to pay for an education or training for a permanent job after the war ends."

And just like that, my days in the Dust Bowl were over.

~

Early the next morning my family and I said our less-than-joyful good-byes standing in our bare and treeless front yard. I could tell Daddy and Mother tried to be happy for me, but their faces betrayed them. They looked ten years older. When Maribelle and I were finally in the car ready to leave for Oklahoma City, she leaned her head out the window and said, "Now, I don't want to tell you what to do with the check I gave you only an hour ago while Molly packed her clothes, Tillman, but give a thought to adding on an extra bedroom for those kids."

"That's the best idea I've heard in a coon's age," Daddy fired back.

I was sure Daddy had a reason for his sudden exhilaration,

only a moment after he had felt so sad. And I thought Maribelle's check must have been enough for a down payment on our farm or to remodel our house and barn.

But I hadn't heard everything yet. On the drive to Oklahoma City, Maribelle told me that only hours before his fatal heart attack, Grandpa Dowden had demanded that she give Daddy half of what the farm would sell for when she finally decided to sell it.

"But," said Maribelle, "what brought your daddy to tears of joy was hearing from me that his grandfather had acknowledged he had always loved Tillman and was sorry he hadn't treated him better when he was growing up. And, Molly, I'm sorry I waited so long to tell your daddy about my promise to his grandfather the day he died so long ago." I took a deep breath and thought, *This kind of news is better late than never.* I was fairly sure I knew what her promise had been.

~

As we sped toward Oklahoma City, Maribelle told me the rest of the story. She had told Daddy about his Grandpa Dowden while she and he sat in the kitchen the night before, talking long after the rest of the house was asleep.

She went on to explain to me as we drove along that her life had taken an entirely different path recently.

When she was offered such a good price for the farm and she looked for the deed, she found it along with a will written in Great-Grandpa Dowden's shaky handwriting dated the day before he died. He never had a chance to take his will to a lawyer and make it legal.

"What did the will say?" I managed to ask at that point.

"The will stipulated that your daddy would be the heir to one-half the amount the farm, livestock, and farm equipment would bring when it was sold. In addition, half of his grandpa's cash in the bank would go to your daddy."

"Cash in the bank?" I asked, interrupting Maribelle again.

Then she said, "It turned out your great-grandfather had a nice nest egg, just as his father had before him. Ran in the family—saving, you know. He had taken his money out of the bank when the stock market crashed in 1929, just before his bank went under. Later he put his money back in another bank where it was safe and grew a little," Maribelle continued. "After I deducted the settlement money I had given your daddy when he left Arkansas, his one-half of that money still amounted to something."

"No wonder I always liked you," I responded, amazed that her true integrity had won out. "You're an honest woman on top of all your other interesting and good qualities."

"Now, now, don't sell me for more than I'm worth," she insisted. "My first husband's folks from out east had left him and me well fixed; and your great-grandpa knew half of his estate would be fair for me. But don't think I wasn't tempted. Remember, I didn't find the will until recently. Truthfully, because I had made a promise to your dying great-grandpa, I just couldn't cheat your daddy."

I couldn't help thinking that Maribelle had been the best person in the world to have stepped into my beloved great-grandmother's shoes. After that I dozed off for a few seconds.

When I woke up I didn't feel awkward, because Maribelle obviously had kept on talking and hadn't noticed that I had fallen asleep.

"Flabbergasting, isn't it?" she said, finally glancing at me. "Think what that means to your daddy, your family—the changes it will make in their lives."

"I know. Oh, how I know!" I replied, now wide awake.

I didn't need a crystal ball to tell me the details, either. I knew that, like other farmers who had inherited their land and worked hard to maintain it, Daddy would take his inheritance and make his farm better. And I believed that from then on, life for the Dowden family in the Dust Bowl would be good. Very good. Knowing that, I finally let unbridled excitement about my own future flood over me.

~

Oklahoma City was huge. In sharp contrast to most farmhouses and yards in southwest Oklahoma, the homes in Oklahoma City were large and well kept, with grass and flowers surrounding them. Several of the buildings downtown were so amazingly tall and looked so crisp and new that I thought I should pinch myself to see if I was dreaming.

~

Maribelle made me comfortable in her small guest bedroom and urged me to feel at home anywhere in her apartment. What a treat to at last live in a big city *and* in a home with electricity, running water, and an indoor toilet with shiny white fixtures and brass faucets. I wanted just to stand and flip the light switch on and off over and over, but I couldn't wait to use the new sparkling bathtub. What a far cry from a metal washtub! Nothing about my arrival was tainted with disappointment.

I even handled well the news in Mother's letter, which Maribelle took from her purse and handed to me when I was settled in my room.

Mother's letter announced she was pregnant, and it stressed that I shouldn't worry, because Tilley, Aaron, and Virginia Sue were pretty independent children and would be good entertainment for the youngest one, Wilson. A little of the new money would be spent on games, toys, coloring books, and such. So Mother would be less busy looking out for the older children, and there would be plenty of time for her to tend to the new baby and do the housekeeping and cooking, too.

~

The next day Maribelle picked me up soon after her work shift ended at 3 p.m. We made it to the aircraft factory employment office with just enough time for me to fill out an application form. The day after that, she picked me up after work to take me to find a waitress job so I would have an income until the defense plant could call me. It felt good to be taken care of so well, and I felt proud to be hired on the spot at the first restaurant where we stopped.

My waitress career was short-lived, however. Within less than a month I was called to work at the plant, and soon I was riding to work every day with my incredible benefactor, Maribelle.

But that wasn't the end of her wonderful generosity. When I received my first paycheck, I asked her to help me find an apartment, and she found one only two blocks from hers. So I continued to ride with Maribelle until a few months later, when I made friends with a young woman who worked in my department at the plant. She owned a car and was looking for a roommate— and a few weeks later she moved in with me. Not long after that, she arranged a blind date for me with her boyfriend's buddy, my future husband, Randal.

Randal was a glib, quick-smile fellow from Minnesota who was stationed at the air base near my apartment and the defense plant. Following our blind date we met often for chats at a nearby soda fountain, where we shared stories about our childhoods and our hopes for the future. He talked of returning to his home near the Wisconsin-Minnesota border when the war was over. "You'd like it there, Molly," he said. "You love trees, and there are trees everywhere up there."

He was an artist with words when he described the remarkable, well-kept, large farmhouses and buildings on each side of the beautiful St. Croix River, which separated Minnesota and Wisconsin. I could almost see the rolling green hills with Holstein cows grazing there; and when he described the deep winter snows surrounding the two-story white houses, the huge nearby red barns, and the towering silos, I longed to see all of that in person. "They must look like the Christmas cards I've seen in drugstores," I exclaimed. "Do they fill the silos with wheat?"

"No," he answered soberly, "they store their money in them."

How charmed I was by his northern accent and his humor. I also was awed by his descriptions of the second- and third-generation American Dutch and Norwegian settlements, and their church lutefisk dinners and smorgasbords—later to be called *buffets*.

We had dated only a couple of months when Randal asked me to marry him. He wanted to set a wedding date within a month because he had heard rumors that he would be sent overseas. I accepted, and the following weekend I took a bus to see my family.

Mother and Daddy had written earlier that they had bought the farm and that Daddy was no longer a tenant farmer for an absentee landlord. He was now a farm owner, and I wanted to see their newly enlarged and remodeled house, and the repairs on the barn and the chicken coop. And I needed to meet my new baby sister, Leah Jane. I also was bursting with excitement at the thought of telling my folks I would marry the soldier from Minnesota, whom I had described so glowingly in my letters.

~

Mother took me aside before I could reveal my plan to marry Randal and confided that Daddy had said right away that I spoke in a different way—"sort of northern," she explained with a smile. And indeed, after I told my family about my plan to marry Randal, Daddy said three times before nightfall, "Yeah, you're going to move up north and talk like them."

Knowing his great-grandfather had lived in Georgia and fought in the Civil War, I tried not to sound "northern." I thought to myself that someday Daddy would go to a place where negative personal feelings about the war between the North and the South were not passed on from generation to generation. When that time should come, I would be glad I had not made a fuss about his feelings.

On Sunday morning before Daddy and I were to leave for the bus station in Westin, something happened that made me doubly glad I had respected his feelings.

I was sitting in my folks' bedroom holding baby Leah Jane for the final time before my departure, and he came into the room and said, "Sister, when the war is over, Randal could find a job in Westin or for sure in Oklahoma City. Then y'all would get to see us every once in a while."

And, as if that hadn't been touching enough, on the way to

the bus station when I was alone with him, another layer of who he was came out when I said, "Mother tells me you go inside the church now and sit with her instead of sitting in the parking lot waiting for the service to end."

"Well, yeah, it's warmer in the church when it's cold and cooler with the electric fans and all when it's hot," he answered, a little embarrassed. "But you know what—I've quit cussing."

Mother had already told me. But I didn't tell him I'd heard that news, and instead, I asked, "Do you miss the swearing?"

"No. No, I don't. I don't think I had meant to blaspheme God anyway. Life has been hard for me since I was a boy, and I think maybe I was just saying, 'Where are you, God?'"

I knew he had truly changed, because he had not said, "Where the *hell* are you, God?"

Final Chapter

Hello, I'm Molly's daughter, Lynn Ruth. Mom nicknamed me Cinny for the color of cinnamon because Grandma Elsa Ruth's red-hair gene came through to me. My brother, James, inherited her red hair as well. Mom says my brother and I not only look like Grandma Elsa Ruth, but we're also as determined. But neither of us has ever killed a snake, not in our house or anywhere else.

A year ago Mom told James and me she wished we would write the final chapter of her story. She said that after she had written everything she could recall about her family's struggle to survive the 1930s Dust Bowl and her transition from country girl to city woman, she felt adrift. And, she admitted, she had not been able to decide how to end her memoir without seeming boastful about the outcome of her life and those of her siblings. "But still, I think people would like to know the final outcome of my story," she concluded.

"I never quite overcame the feeling of disbelief that it all could have happened to me, a skinny Okie," she said that day after James and I quizzed her about her life after Thistleway. And that was how she truly felt. Still in disbelief after so many years!

In her senior years Mom was diagnosed with chronic

obstructive pulmonary disease, and she suffered numerous lung infections due in part to the damage to her respiratory system from untreated dust pneumonia in her youth. Later in her life, CT scans revealed that the old damage to her lungs was getting worse and she needed to be put on a regimen of inhaled medications and periodically prescribed antibiotics. She remained active with housekeeping, daily one-mile walks, weekly ballroom dancing, and cheering at the home games for the Minnesota Women's Gopher basketball team. But two months ago, she waited too long before alerting her doctor to prescribe antibiotics for a lung infection, and she passed away—just five months after our father's sudden death. And since the final part of her memoir was still unfinished, James and I decided to take on the task of writing Mom's last chapter. But be forewarned: we will summarize, not dramatize.

In regard to Mom's five siblings, none of them became farmers or married farmers. Her sisters, Virginia Sue and Leah Jane, both became business owners. Brother Tilley was a traveling salesman, so to speak, and Aaron owned a car sales business. Wilson, the youngest brother, earned a PhD and taught college-level and postgraduate classes, and to date he has authored six published academic books.

Mom's parents, our Grandpa and Grandma Dowden, remained a long while on the Oklahoma farm. During a recurrence of dust storms in the early 1950s, Grandpa's respiratory problems worsened and Grandma's iritis returned. When another spate of dust storms returned in the 1970s, they decided to sell the farm, and, by then in their sixties, they moved to Oklahoma City, where Mom's two sisters and brother Wilson were living. Grandpa's respiratory system deteriorated as he aged, and he passed away at age seventy-six. Grandma sold their house in an Oklahoma City suburb and moved into an apartment, where she lived independently and contentedly without aftereffects of the iritis she had suffered in her younger years. She died during a brief hospitalization when she was ninety-four.

~

As to how Mom's life unfolded in Oklahoma City, she quickly advanced from trainee to first-class rating at the defense plant, where she riveted various sections of the military's renowned workhorse planes, first the C-47 and later the tail section of the C-54. Interestingly, some historians have proclaimed that the assembly line workers' excellent productivity in our defense plants was an essential part of America's success in the war. I recall Mom once said, "Many of the men in the Oklahoma City defense plant were older, and the women ranged from older to just out of high school, but we all focused our full attention on our assembly line work after the starting whistle sounded. We simply couldn't do it any other way. Our loved ones overseas deserved that from us."

It turned out our father never did get shipped overseas. Until the war ended, he and Mom lived in a rented white picket-fenced bungalow not far from Mom's work and our father's military base.

Mom was four weeks pregnant with me, her first, when they moved north to our father's home area, a small town near St. Paul, Minnesota. Our father took advantage of the GI Bill and earned his college degree, while Mom stayed home to care for James and me. Her social life consisted of PTA meetings, coffee klatches, book clubs, and church groups. Her hobbies were reading, northern cooking (especially Dutch and Norwegian), and sewing. Sewing was her favorite, actually, and she made clothes for me and James as well as for herself.

Mom received many compliments on her dressmaking skills

and was told frequently that she wore her designs so well she ought to be a fashion model. She already knew that some of the Miss Americas had been tall since World War II. Bess Myerson, for example, was five foot ten; BeBe Shopp was five foot nine, an inch taller than my mom. So Mom thought, why not give modeling a try, just for fun, not a career.

Our father, always supportive of our mother, told her she certainly should look into the local modeling schools; and no sooner said than done, she was commuting by bus to modeling classes in downtown Minneapolis.

In modeling school she was delighted one day when the petite, pretty instructor said, "Let me explain the emergence of the new prototype for our postwar woman. She is tall. She is feminine. Short and curvy women are making room for their lovely, statuesque sisters. Together, short and tall women served in the military and worked in defense factories during the war—both jobs, up until then, thought to be men's work. But we proved that what we can do, we do well."

Mom had written in her notes that the entire class applauded the pretty and petite instructor when she finished her pep talk.

Soon after Mom finished modeling school, it became clear to her that the country was filled with optimism and that spirit spilled over into the garment industry. This was evidenced by a flurry of fashion shows in the Twin Cities, St. Paul and Minneapolis, and she set out to make use of her recent training. She taught classes at the same modeling school she had attended, she modeled on TV, and her picture appeared several times in St. Paul papers advertising clothing for local stores. She also did in-store modeling as well as modeling on runways. At last, the young Molly May Dowden's childhood pastime perusing dog-eared catalogs and wishing to model pretty clothes had come true.

As a result of her professional modeling experiences, she was asked to speak about posture, poise, and grooming to local high school home economics classes during their sewing units. And in the summertime she judged beauty contests in small Minnesota and Wisconsin towns.

She reveled in that contact with teenagers and morphed to the next stage of her "becoming." At age forty she registered as a college freshman and commuted to the university. In three and a half years, she earned a bachelor's degree, graduating with honors, including the American Association of University Women's Award. After graduation, she immediately went on to earn her master's while also teaching full time.

During the twenty-one years she taught high-school English, she also taught one summer at a college in England. Another summer, she took postgraduate classes in England, and the following summer, classes in Greece. In addition, after they retired, she and our father traveled throughout the United States and many countries abroad.

Not long after they finished their travels, I discovered that Mom had a keen interest in Chinese culture. That interest had been spawned in her youth when she read Pearl Buck's novels. So I invited her to go with me to China on my next business trip. She was such a trooper at seventy-five that I invited her to go to China with me again a year later. And she did.

~

As per Mom's wishes, James and I buried most of her ashes next to our father in Minnesota. The destination for the remainder of her ashes was up to James and me, both of us living in different parts of the country. "Find a place you think would be meaningful to both of you—and me," she had once said with her familiar wry smile.

So, a few days ago, we traveled to the farm in southwest Oklahoma where Mom grew up. We met with her brother and sister, Tilley and Virginia. They had visited the farm in recent times and had figured out where the old house and barn once stood.

Uncle Tilley and Aunt Virginia showed us the area where Mom had played school in the shade of the house or spent time reading there when the weather was nice.

James delivered a brief eulogy before we sprinkled smidgeons of Mom in her former reading place. We also distributed the scant remainder in the front yard, where she had played hopscotch on cool mornings and where her bare feet had felt the scorch of the afternoon summer heat. Then the four of us stood gazing silently across the once-upon-a-time beige prairie, now green with crops. The only sounds of life, aside from an occasional passing car, were the faraway sounds of farm machinery and a dog's bark.

"Yeah, the old house, the barn, and the chicken coop are long gone, and our old land has been absorbed into one huge farm," said Uncle Tilley, reinforcing our awareness of the difference made by time, better weather, better farming technology, and diminishing small-scale farming.

"Good change is good," Aunt Virginia spoke up.

True, I thought to myself as I nodded in agreement with her comment. And now only photographs and Mom's stories remain to remind her family and those interested in learning of the southwest's desperately hard economic times, drought, and dust storms. For James and me, Mom's memoir honors the Dust Bowl survivors and the noble folks who cared about those less fortunate than themselves during our country's worst hard times.

~

After setting a plan to meet at a Thistleway restaurant for dinner, James, Aunt Virginia, Uncle Tilley, and I slowly walked the few feet to our cars.

As James drove the two of us away in our rental car, he said quietly, "While we were looking across the field at the pasture where Mom carried the heavy buckets of water from the well to the house, the words of a philosopher, whose name escapes me right now, came to me."

"Yes, James, what were they?" I asked.

"'That which does not kill us makes us stronger,'" he answered, and neither of us said a word for a moment.

But I was thinking, and I imagined James was, too, that Mom's difficult life—being the oldest child in a poor family during the Dust Bowl and the Great Depression—had made her strong. She overcame some unique hardships in this place—all of which played a huge role in shaping the shy, young Molly into the mother, teacher, and person she became. And I knew then why we had chosen to bring a part of Mom back to this place where she grew up.

In Memoriam

To my brother William Jr., who was in many ways Tilley in this story. He passed away a few days after I finished the final draft of this book. Happy trails, JR.

Author's grade-school class picture, with most of the girls in flour sack dresses. Author in back row, second from right.

Author modeling a designer suit in the 1950s.

Author as a teacher in 1990.